Teeth
The First Bite

Chele Cooke

Teeth: The First Bite / Chele Cooke. -- 1st ed.
ISBN: 978-1505360066

For Rhian

For getting vampires into my head again.
You supported and helped me
with each bite I took of this story.
I couldn't have done it without you.

Alice & Ben
Enjoy this bite
of the story

1

The bathroom tap was leaking again. A tang of rust from the pipes filled the air, pulsing through his senses with each resonating drip. He rolled onto his side, groping around his waist for the blankets. It was too cold to consider getting out of bed. His stomach growled and churned, begging for food, but he couldn't think of a single thing that sounded appetising.

Each drop from the tap pounded through his head, and Thomas buried his face against the pillow. In his state of drunkenness the night before, he must have forgotten to close the bathroom door, keeping the noise at bay. The pipe gurgled at the constant flow of water. It seemed louder than usual.

Maybe that was just the headache talking.

Thomas couldn't even remember if the night out had been worth it. His stomach was churning, his head pounding, and the smell of rust in the air both turned his stomach and gnawed at him in hunger. The fifth drink—or perhaps the sixth—was the last he could remember. He groped forwards with his leg, trying to locate a blanket. He could only imagine that later on he'd be told tales of how hilarious he'd been in some venture or another.

His foot, in its blind search for the blanket, slid across something wet and sticky. Grimacing, Thomas groaned and retreated, wondering if he'd spilt something. Though, now he thought about the wet patch near the bottom of the mattress, he realised something else: this wasn't his mattress. It was hard, lumpy, and had a definite sag under his hip.

He'd gone home with someone. He'd left the bar with someone who apparently didn't own a blanket and also had a leaky tap. Now he knew exactly what the stories would be about when he got to work. Perhaps he'd found someone nice, someone with long and beautiful dark hair, copper skin that sometimes seemed to glow.

Thomas flinched and squeezed his eyes closed tighter. He half hoped that it would remove the picture he was quickly getting in his head, a picture he knew wouldn't be real. The other half hoped that he'd be able to remember the girl when he saw her asleep next to him. She wouldn't be the one he had wanted for months now, the one he constantly pictured when his mother asked when he'd stop thinking about work and find a girl. But she would be nice. At least, he hoped.

Thomas opened his eyes.

Then he began screaming.

Splatters of blood covered the bare walls. A pool of it had spread so far across the concrete floor that it was soaking into the edge of the mattress, creeping through the material. Fingers drifted inches above the pool, arms swaying as calmly as willow branches over a red lake.

Thomas launched himself across the mattress away from the blood and away from the corpse hanging upside down above it. It had to be a corpse. True, he'd not yet completed his medical internship, but he knew how much blood a body could lose and this was definitely more than that. Far more than that. He tumbled off the edge of the mattress and onto the concrete on the other side, pressing his back against the rough brick and drawing his knees up to his chest. The distance only made the sight worse. He could see more of it now. He could see more of her.

The corpse was a woman. She had been suspended from a beam across the small, bare room, a rope knotted so tightly around her bare ankles that the skin beneath was raw and bleeding, her feet black and blue. She wore nothing but her underwear and thin streams of blood wove their way across her skin from numerous long, thin slashes across her body. Her skin looked even paler against the dark blood. Even though she'd clearly been hanging there for some time the blood hadn't stopped dribbling from the cuts.

The pipe gurgled.

No, *she* gurgled.

Thomas's gaze shot to the woman's face. He expected to see lifeless eyes staring blankly ahead but he was wrong. She was watching him. Pale green eyes blinked. Choking on his own breath, Thomas covered his mouth as the urge to be sick boiled up into his throat. He could taste bile, more acrid than he had ever tasted. Four hooks held her mouth as wide as it could go, blood dribbling along the shining silver metal. A fifth bar joined them, pierced through the centre of her tongue, pulling it out at a grotesque angle. She couldn't talk, couldn't move. She probably would have been able to scream at first but now, having lost so much blood, all she could do was gurgle.

Thomas scrambled to his feet. He tripped across the room and grasped the door handle with both hands. He wrenched it toward him. A cry of frustration and terror slipped out as the handle came off in his hand.

He glanced back in desperation. She was still watching him.

He looked around, fingers trembling around the useless door handle. There was no other way out of the room. There were no windows, not even a ventilation duct. He was trapped in a room with a woman who had been tortured and left to bleed to death. Who knew what would happen next? Would the person who'd done this to the woman come back? Had they called the police and framed it on him? He didn't remember the night before, he had no alibi. His friends would know he'd left the bar, probably that he'd left with a woman. This woman.

That was it. They'd framed him and spiked his drink. It was why he couldn't remember the night before. Even if he'd woken in time, there were drugs that left the system quickly. That had to be why he had such an atrocious hangover. It was probably the perfect crime. Blame the door handle on his own stupidity. Case closed.

Thomas froze, staring at the door. No, it wasn't closed. The case wasn't closed because the woman was still alive. Whatever sick bastard had put him in here probably hadn't thought she would survive this long.

Thomas glanced uneasily at her. She blinked. Dropping the handle with a clatter on the concrete he stepped timidly toward her. He grimaced and navigated his way around the blood. He covered his nose and mouth against the smell as another heave brought the bile into his throat. He crouched down.

"I'm…"

He glanced up toward the rope around her ankles and then to the device in her mouth. If he untied the rope she'd fall onto the concrete. She'd lost so much blood that she wouldn't be able to break her fall and he wouldn't be able to catch her. The device would destroy her mouth completely if she knocked it as she hit the ground. It might even kill her if that spike hit wrong.

"I'm going to try to take this out."

She shook her head. Pale blond hair skimmed the surface of the blood sending a ripple through the pool.

Thomas stared at her. She couldn't be serious that she didn't want it out. He knew it was dangerous. The bar through her tongue would be staunching a greater flow of what little blood she had left. No, it had to come out. He couldn't get her down without removing it.

"I'll be careful," he insisted, reaching out. "Don't worry, I have…"

She shook her head more forcefully, a gurgle of dissent bubbling in her throat. Thomas pulled his hand back.

"I don't know what else to do."

"Nu-heng," she gurgled.

His eyes narrowed, and his thumb came straight to his mouth, nibbling at the nail. He got to his feet, pacing back and forth at the edge of the blood pool. She was pretty, no, beautiful. She was the kind of beautiful that pulled you in. He could see why he'd left with her, and what attracted someone to want her so desperately they did this. Her eyes were pale, but they had an odd sort of fire. She looked at him the same way Paige at the coffee shop looked at him, and his stomach clenched.

"I can't leave you like this."

"Yes you can, and you will."

The door had opened as silently as breath. Thomas jumped away from the woman, tripping backwards into the wall. He slid down it and looked up into the cold blue gaze of an older man. His eyes seemed paler than they should be, like someone had extracted half the colour, leaving them almost grey. He regarded Thomas for a moment before stepping further into the room, rounding the woman and taking no care to avoid the blood. His boots sucked from the floor with a squelch. Thomas wanted to be sick.

The man wasn't particularly tall, nor built, and Thomas's gaze flickered to the woman, wondering how in the world he'd gotten her up there on his own. He opened his mouth, but no sound found his throat. What if there were more of them? The man trailed his fingers across the back of the woman's bare shoulders and smiled with pale lips.

"Have you drank?"

Thomas shuffled away from him and peered up with wide, blank eyes.

"What?"

The man rolled his eyes and stepped up onto the mattress, red footprints across the material. He crouched down and took Thomas's chin in a vice grip. The man's pale eyes were inches from his, taking in every detail of his face.

"Have – you – drank?" he asked again. Each word dripped in disdain, and Thomas shook his head as much as the man's grasp would allow.

"Drank what? There's nothing in here," he breathed.

Glancing over his shoulder at the woman, the man's gaze returned pointedly to Thomas. Thomas froze, his gaze flickering between the man and... and *her.*

"You can't... You're... No!"

The man rolled his eyes and shoved Thomas back against the wall away from him. He was on his feet in a single motion, quicker than he could think to follow his movements and get the better of him. Thomas sat against the wall, rubbing the pain from the back of his head where he'd hit the brick. The door was barely open, but maybe he could get to it. He drew his knees up to his chest, keeping a cautious gaze on the man as he pushed himself, inch by inch, up the wall, ready to run.

The man no longer paid any attention to him. He was looking at the woman. He leaned down and grasped her by the hair, tugging her up as if she were as light as a rag doll.

"You break their rules. You make me do this to you," he crooned in a voice that verged on loving disappointment. "And you leave me with a fucking vegetarian?"

2

The smoke rose in a swirling column and bloomed above Spencer's head. Heavy clouds that promised rain blocked the last of the stars, what little could be seen through the haze of the city lights. A red dawn spread up from the horizon tingeing everything it touched in a peach glow.

Spencer sucked in another lungful from his cigarette and flicked the end of the butt, sending the ash into the grass. Holding the sweet smoke behind his lips and drawing it down into his lungs, he relished the feeling before he sent it out in a perfect spiral stream.

"Cutting it fine, aren't you?"

Spencer didn't need to look over his shoulder to place the voice. That voice was as ingrained in his head as his own. He'd been around it for over five years now and he didn't want to think it would ever truly go away. His chuckle sent a cloud of misty breath out into the cool air and he pointed his cigarette at the horizon.

"Closest I get to sunrise," he said.

They stood and watched the slow progression of colour before the sun showed its face. Spencer smoked his cigarette, and August turned to watch him.

"I do not see the point of your little habit, Spencer."

Spencer glanced at the cigarette in his hand.

"It won't kill me."

"The fact it is not lethal is not a reason to continue."

"It's a habit, August, nothing more."

"A habit you could just as easily discard. The nicotine has no hold on you."

Spencer sighed and looked down at his cigarette again. There was something about August's words that drained the enjoyment out of the little stick. He had already brought it half way to his lips but he dropped his hand, tapping his thumb against the side of his thigh. He turned his attention to his companion instead. August's pale hair shone despite the lack of moonlight, and his pale blue eyes glinted like the absent stars.

"You do this every morning," August noted, a small pull at the corner of his lips.

It wasn't a surprise that August had watched him. The older man seemed to know everything that went on. Spencer had never seen him surprised, despite the number of odd tales that passed through their doors.

"I'm sure you have your own little rituals when no one is around."

August looked at him then. Despite his young features, there was something old about August Caine. Spencer had always noticed it and it seemed more pronounced in the pre-dawn, the light drawing his pale age from his skin. Or perhaps it was the job he'd been performing downstairs which made him so much older. Spencer took a drag of his cigarette and flicked the butt out onto the grass, leaving the glowing embers to be devoured by dew.

With the sweet smoke filtering away, Spencer picked up another scent. He looked down at the wooden beams of the balcony. Sure enough, a line of bloody footprints led to their position.

"You saw the new one? That's where you were tonight?"

August followed his gaze and smirked upon the sight of his boot tread against the yellowing wood. It was a cruel smirk of absolute amusement. Spencer had seen it many times, mostly before August killed. Though they all mostly hunted separately to avoid attracting attention, he'd seen August kill more than any of the others. He was the perfect hunter. Skilled, patient, and utterly ruthless.

"Quite petrified," August mused. "Though I remember you experiencing the same horror in the beginning."

"I woke up in an unfamiliar room with my one night stand hanging from the ceiling."

"Any lesson is learned faster when you have an example to follow."

Spencer scoffed and looked away. The way August spoke about it amused him, like turning and accepting their new life was a maths equation to be solved. However, August was right. The horror of seeing what happened to someone who broke the rules had stuck with him. It had been a good motivator to ensure he never broke them himself. Though unlike others, he'd never really come close to considering it. He had everything he wanted here.

The very fact he existed had been proof of a broken law. No one was to be turned without permission, and permission was rarely given. Cleo was not the first to break that particular law. Though he'd not been around to see it, there had been many who broke it over the decades. The boy they were keeping downstairs at that very moment was the first new vampire he'd seen in his five short years.

It was a pity. He'd liked Cleo. She'd been there for him almost as much as August had in the beginning. The man next to him had been assigned, ordered to help him through his transformation once his maker had been bled for his crime, the sire bonds destroyed. Eventually a closer relationship had been born from his training with August, but in the beginning he had been cold and distant, only doing what he must, teaching him how to survive and little more. The older man had almost relished the panic and hardship Spencer had suffered. He enjoyed mocking the ways Spencer had failed those first few times. Cleo, on the other hand, had chosen to help him because she had wanted to. She was the gentle guidance to August's stern demands.

"Will she be given reprieve?" Spencer asked.

August stepped forward and grasped the railing that surrounded the balcony. He leaned forward, looking down at the grass. Letting out a growl, he kicked the toe of his boot against the wood in a steady, absent rhythm.

"No."

Spencer's eyes narrowed as he watched August.

"Why? Didn't she…"

"The only thing that saved her last time was the pure amusement William provided," August cut him off.

"You mean the wedding?"

Whatever anguish or annoyance August felt about having to bleed Cleo was instantly hidden by a mask of pure joy. He stood up straight and turned around, leaning back on the railing, crossing his arms over his chest.

"You would have given anything to see such a show," he

said. "Cleo finished the transformation before anyone else even knew about William. Before they could reach him, or Cleo could be bled to break the bonds, he had used his twilight to run off to his own wedding. He slaughtered some seventy guests before moving onto his bride."

Spencer leaned on the railing next to him.

"I've heard the stories."

"Well then you'll know that such instinct has not been seen in a long time."

Spencer rocked to the side and bumped his shoulder against August's.

"I'm sure you were worse."

August tried to look humble, but his eyes gave away his pleasure at the praise. He patted his hand against Spencer's thigh.

"I took time, like you," he explained fondly. "Not many are so ready for such a change. Cleo picked a good one with him."

The open door beckoned to them. Spencer could feel the heat of the sunrise on his shoulders and the way it spread through his skin as if he were standing in the mid-summer sun. It wouldn't be long before they would need to be inside, but they had a few minutes. He didn't want to move and risk his questions going unanswered. August was always loath to talk where he would be overheard. Spencer had never known anyone so meticulous.

"This new one then? He won't save her?"

August shook his head in disdain.

"He hasn't even drank yet."

"It's jarring," Spencer insisted. "Coming to terms with it all. He will."

"It's been three days."

"He doesn't remember that."

The smile was back on August's lips.

"You only took two."

A sense of pride flooded through him. Spencer pushed off the railing to take a last glimpse of the pink horizon. It saddened him almost every morning. By each evening, however, the sadness was forgotten at the sight of the midnight ink that swallowed the sky.

"You can't all be as perfect as me," he said with a wicked grin.

August sighed and shook his head in mock sadness.

"No, I suppose we can't."

"Have you considered telling him?" Spencer asked. "How long he's been here? What's happening to him?"

He remembered those days. He hadn't been able to at first but now he could look back and push through the confusion that had clouded him. The pain and nausea like a particularly bad hangover. He hadn't realised that he was dying. It had taken a while to believe it, even after August had told him so. Believing it and acting on it, however, were two different things, especially when acting on it meant killing someone.

"He won't remember until he's ready."

"But it might speed the process."

"That does not matter," August said. "The orders have been handed down. Cleo is to be bled. Whether the boy is turned now or not will not change that."

August and Cleo were close and had been for a long time. They were amongst the oldest of their group, only beaten in age by Charles. The bitterness in August's snarl was clear, and he looked away from him.

"Charles can't be persuaded?"

August scoffed.

"When have you ever known that man to change his mind,

Spencer?" he sneered. "The order has been given. His rules are all he cares about, and if I do not perform this, another will."

"Maybe you could change things?" Spencer asked quietly, checking the open door behind them. "People like you, you know that."

"The instinct to survive is stronger than personal affections, you will learn that," he said with brisk dismissal. "It is the same with that boy downstairs. I have done this enough to know that once survival instinct kicks in nothing will stop them. Cleo will be gone soon, and the sooner the better."

There was no fighting the matter. August had seen far more new ones than he had. Spencer wondered if the older man thought him weak, wanting to be kind and understanding to the new one. It wasn't that, not really. He had no interest in the man below their floors. He simply wanted it out of the way. The faster the transition was completed, the faster August would return. There was something off about him, though he couldn't place his finger on what. He wondered if it was Cleo's involvement. It had to be sad, letting her go, knowing that she had broken the rules they'd lived contently by for so long.

Spencer laid his hand on August's shoulder. The older man didn't even look at him. He stared through the open doorway, his eyes betraying his preoccupation with what was happening below.

"I can do it if you want."

August looked at him then, a calm resignation that hardened his attractive features.

"No. Cleo has her price to pay," he said. "And I have mine."

August stepped away from him. The moment the contact was broken between them, Spencer felt the warmth slip from his fingers.

15

"I don't understand."

In the doorway, his silhouette illuminated by the dim light, he paused. He turned his head just enough that Spencer could see the outline of his nose, his thin lips pressed together in a tight line.

"Thanks to our laws, Spencer, you'll never have to."

Without another word, and before Spencer had the time to question him further, August was gone, leaving him alone on the balcony with the rising sun.

3

The stone steps leading down into the basement were sticky with blood. The footsteps from his last visit led the way from the locked room and August did little to avoid them. No doubt the new one would assume the blood was on his shoes from when he'd strung Cleo up in the room. He'd never suspect that this wasn't the first visit.

The young were idiotic.

Personally, he didn't like the basement. It screamed of clichés. However, it was the easiest room to clean and he had no inclination to start redecorating. That was Cleo's job, her love.

Correction, it used to be her job.

Her scent was everywhere. The smell of her blood ran so deep that it felt like his own sometimes. He'd known the day would come. Deep down, like the blood, he'd always known. Cleo was too impulsive. All his hard work, all his planning and careful consideration, and she just couldn't wait. Sometimes it worked in her favour, like with William, but others... He could only protect her for so long, despite how hard he had tried. He had cleaned up the mess of each indiscretion. He had hidden the evidence and kept her hands clean. And every time he did, she had hated him a little more.

It was too late to protect her this time, even if he'd tried. She'd brought the man back with her. He had been stumbling and already sick with her blood. Near enough everyone had seen, and those who hadn't had heard about it as the young gossiped in the halls, the salacious story passed from ear to ear. There would be no chance to kill the new one before anyone knew. He'd offered, of course. Many died in the transformation and he had proven time and time again that he could lie. She was so fierce in her refusal that he knew: She hadn't chosen this new one because she couldn't hold back. She'd chosen him because she couldn't hold on.

She wanted to die and it killed him.

August wanted to think that she wouldn't have known that he would be the one selected to dispose of her but the thought clawed at him. She'd seen him dispose of others who broke the rules under Charles' orders. She'd waited to hear the reports, to offer her suggestions on ridding them of the body. That it would be him chosen this time was only fair, wasn't it? After he'd killed so many others for her.

There was another way, other methods he could have used if he'd wanted. She'd probably have enjoyed them. She'd always been fascinated with the others, even though they rarely saw them around here. However, their rules were clear. They were to keep their distance, they were not to disrupt the careful balance that had been created over decades. The young didn't even know. They continued on with their lives none the wiser to what existed outside their own little radius. It was better that way, he supposed. The young were foolhardy and believed themselves invincible. They would only get themselves killed if they knew. Not that they didn't get themselves killed anyway, but once again, August was there to clean it up.

He seemed to clean up everyone's messes. The eternal fucking janitor.

He paused at the door, his hand already on the handle. The new one was pacing and, from the tacky pull of each foot coming off the concrete, he'd ventured into the blood. Probably another attempt to free Cleo, not that she'd have allowed it. He was bonded to her and he would have had little choice but to obey her. Anything to make her happy, even if it meant letting her die.

August pushed the door open and took in the scene. He made no effort to be quiet, not like the last time. The man turned to face him. He was paler than before and the scent of vomit and fever radiated from him. The smell of the food forced from the man's stomach sent a wave of nausea through his own. He took a breath and stepped in, closing the door behind him. The handle was still attached. He hadn't tried escaping again.

"Have you drank?"

The young man took a step along the wall, careful to avoid the pool of blood that now covered most of the small room. He left a brown footprint in his wake.

August moved into the room, and the man leapt further away.

"I said, have you drank?"

"Stop asking me that!"

He glanced at Cleo. Her skin was greying, her ribs showing clearly under her chest. Even her bra looked a size too big. The bleeding was taking effect. After three days, he wasn't surprised. If anything, he was surprised she had lasted this long. Most didn't, but then most who suffered this fate were young and impulsive.

Cleo was not young, though he couldn't say she wasn't impulsive. She had known better, she simply didn't care.

She held him with a defiant stare. Her eyes, which had once been as bright as leaves in summer, were now a faded mint green. Even her hair seemed to have lost some of its colour. He turned away.

"What would you prefer I ask you?"

The young man faltered, staring blankly at him. August crouched and ran a single finger through the blood, stroking the rough concrete beneath.

"What is your name?"

"T-Thomas."

August nodded.

"Why are you doing this?" Thomas asked. "Why me? Why… why her?"

Cleo caught his gaze again, and this time it was August who was lost for an answer. Getting to his feet, he ran his index finger idly along his bottom lip leaving a trail of congealing blood across the flesh. He took a breath in past his lips, shivering at the pleasure that rippled through him as the taste of blood clung to the back of his throat. He grinned as Thomas licked across his bottom lip, shuddered, and turned away.

"I do this because I must. However, I cannot claim responsibility for choosing you."

Thomas's gaze followed his nod toward Cleo, who watched the younger man with a sad longing.

"You're lying."

The warmth of Cleo's skin worried August as he trailed his

fingertips along the ridges of her spine. She was coming closer. At long last, death was creeping in. After so many years of chasing her, it finally had her in its clutches. Fixing a mocking smile onto his lips, he leaned around her, peering past her hip at the young man.

"Do you believe that I'm lying? Or would you simply prefer if I were?"

"What do you mean?"

The backs of Cleo's fingers brushed against his trouser leg, and when August looked down, she'd left a streaky smear across the pale material. He took her hand, holding it in both of his own as he kissed her knuckles. She whimpered and sighed.

"Tell me you feel nothing for this woman," he said, gazing at Thomas through the gaps in Cleo's fingers. "Honestly now."

"Why should I?"

"Why, indeed?" he pressed. "You only met her…"

"Two nights ago."

August's gaze was drawn down to Cleo. She was smiling. Well, she was smiling as much as was possible with the contraption holding her mouth open as wide as it would go. Even looking like this, knowing she would hate him more than he knew possible, he longed to let her down. He could easily jump across the mattress and snap the boy's neck. She seemed to know what he was thinking, and shook her head. He closed his eyes for a moment then turned away.

"You remember, then?"

"Yes. What's that got to do with it?"

Waving a hand dismissively, he kissed the back of Cleo's fingers again. They tasted metallic and familiar, and make his heart ache.

"Let me make my move," he whispered. "Let me save you. I'll do anything."

She shook her head.

"I'd get you a puppy if you asked me." His smile was wicked, though he didn't feel it. She let out a gurgle of a laugh. Still, she shook her head.

August clutched her hand tighter against his lips.

"You didn't answer me," August reminded the boy. "Tell me. If you only met this woman two days ago, why do you feel for her?"

"Because I'm human!" Thomas snapped. "And you've left her bleeding."

"And yet you didn't take her down?"

Thomas stared at him. His mouth opened and closed, his breath coming faster. August stepped forward, finally releasing Cleo's hand.

"In two days of her hanging here, bleeding to death, you never thought to let her down and help heal her?"

What little of the boy's stomach contents were left churned in a low grumble. August wrinkled his nose.

"She didn't want me to."

"And you listened to what she said."

"She… she didn't say it. She couldn't with that thing in her mouth."

August chuckled.

"My, my, that is interesting. A woman telling you things psychically."

Thomas didn't answer. He hunched over, lowering himself into a crouch. He rubbed his hands back and forth over his neck. It had been so long, but August remembered the frustration. He hadn't believed. No one believed at first.

"What's happening to me?" Thomas moaned.

"You're dying."

That caught his attention. The young man lifted his head, fingers frozen in his hair, and he stared open mouthed.

"She turned you. Your body is dying. You can stop it, but only if you drink."

"You're…"

"Lying? No."

"Crazy!"

"Perhaps, but that doesn't stop me from being right."

Thomas gave a bitter laugh and shook his head. On his feet again, he retreated into the corner of the room.

"Turned? What does that even mean? I'm not dying."

"She smells good, right?"

The shake of the boy's head was too frantic to be believed. Denial was a common stage. August had learned long ago that the stages psychologists said the grieving went through were true. Only, they didn't imagine that the stages still occurred when death was not the only option.

"Thomas, you have a choice. You can either die in this room, or you can listen to me and save yourself. By drinking you will turn."

"Die here? But…"

"For you to live, you must drink, which will kill her. There is no option for you both to survive now. You will turn or you will die."

"What do you mean, turn?"

This boy was slower than most and it was infuriating. Cleo should have at least chosen someone intelligent, interesting. William was a brute but at least he was entertaining. August couldn't see any redeeming factors in this boy. Maybe he'd kill the boy off once this was done. It wouldn't be difficult. Maybe the others would be glad of it. He could get into talks with them, even. Charles wouldn't even need to know.

"I think you already know," he said, his face a mask of cool indifference. "Not many creatures need to drink blood in order to survive."

"If you say what I think you're going to, I'll kill you right now."

August laughed.

"I would love to see you try." He paused, straightening himself up. "Vampire."

4

The harder he scrubbed, the more ingrained the stains became. They seeped into his skin, delved into the cracks and crevices. The deeper they went, the less he wanted to get rid of them, which had only made him scrub his skin all the harder. Turning away from her constant watch over him, Thomas brought his legs up to his chest and rested his forehead on his knees.

The man had proved how easily he could take him down. Apart from the ache in his shoulder where he'd hit the floor, the blonde man hadn't even hurt him. Before Thomas had been able to throw a single punch, the man had swiped his foot around his ankle and Thomas was face down on the floor. Face down in the blood. It had all been too fast. He remembered moving, trying to throw the punch, and then it was over.

He wrapped his arms around his legs. It was too insane. The man was toying with him. Thomas idly wondered if there was a camera hidden in the room watching how long it would take for him to break and try to save himself. The woman wouldn't last much longer and he wondered if it only worked while she was alive.

No, it was ridiculous.

Thomas brought his hand up, resting his chin in the crook of his thumb. He nibbled on the side of his finger, swiping his tongue back and forth across the flesh. The man was obviously insane. Sadistic even. He was lying to him. The lack of food and water was making him delusional. He wasn't dying, he was dehydrated.

How long had it been since he'd had a proper drink? One of those great coffees from the café on the corner. Maybe Paige would put that half shot in it for him, the way he liked.

Thomas glanced over at the woman. She was different to Paige in every way. Where she was blonde, Paige had long dark hair, bronzed skin where this woman was pale. All the colour was draining away with the blood, leaving her in shades of grey.

She was still beautiful.

She gurgled again.

Thomas looked over his shoulder. Her eyes were wide, encouraging. Thomas paused. Then he looked down.

His hands were covered in the dark cold blood except for a small patch on the side of his index finger. A patch he had licked clean. Thomas swallowed the lump constricting his throat. He stared at the spot, willing himself to claw the blood from his tongue. Instead he swiped his thumb across the side of his finger, covering the patch with a brown smear.

"No."

"Kuh-ning."

Thomas crawled across the mattress toward her, peering closer. He'd long given up his attempts not to go through her blood. So little of the floor remained clean that it had become impossible to avoid.

"What?"

"Yawh kuh-ning."

He could smell the blood as it dribbled from the cuts in her skin. It smelled fresher than the rest. It smelled better.

His breath caught in his throat. The faster he tried to pull air in, the harder he spluttered and coughed. Digging his fingers into the side of the mattress, Thomas heaved. Blood swam in his vision. The pool on the floor was writhing before him and his head swam with it.

Vomit splattered across the floor. Ripples of blood swayed outward and converged on the mixture. Thomas instinctively brought his hand to his mouth and the moment his blood smeared hand touched his lips the taste of bile was gone, replaced with rust and raw steak. His stomach clenched in spasm, and Thomas rocked his shoulders, urging himself to get it over with. He squeezed his eyes shut, trying to burp, to bring it up.

"Gwink."

He lifted his head. Looking back at him, the smallest of smiles alight in her eyes, she lifted a limp hand. She faltered, her arm drooping with the effort, but she offered again, reaching towards him as far as she could. Thomas took her hand.

"I…" He shook his head. "I don't believe in this. This is…"

She coughed and nodded.

"I don't want you to die."

He didn't even know why, apart from humanity. He didn't know her. He didn't even remember meeting her, not really. He could see her face, shining and warm, beautiful, but he couldn't remember what was said or even how they met. All he knew was that he wanted her around. He wanted her protected and him to be the one to do it. He wanted her to live. Thomas clasped her hand tighter. He needed her to live.

"Gwink."

She wiggled her fingers in his grasp, and he gazed at the smears his dirty hands had made against her greying skin. A thin, pure, drop of blood was carving a path over the browned stains, a maroon line, just visible on the inside of her wrist. Lifting her hand, he shuffled forward on his knees. Blood soaked through his jeans, clinging to his skin. The tip of his tongue caught the errant drop.

He couldn't pull his gaze from her face. His lips found the blood instinctively, taste it even before his tongue found each drop. She watched him, joy and longing in her eyes. Nodding with encouragement with each taste, she sighed in pleasure as his lips travelled further up her arm, honing in on the slight pulse at the crook of her elbow. He found one of the bleeding cuts there and sucked it dry. She liked that the best.

Her name was Cleo, he knew that now. With every taste, he could feel his lips curving around the name, the way just the tip of her tongue would touch her upper lip as she told it to him. The smile was there, in her eyes and her cheeks as she touched his arm and moved in closer to be heard over the thump of music in the dark club. She drank him in with a single word, and he could only hope to ever get that close.

Her skin was warm, much warmer than his fingers as they reached up and grasped her waist, holding her in place. His tongue travelled over her shoulder, her collarbone, the curve underneath her breast where the bra was too loose and hung from her chest. With each lick she became warmer. Each taste had her burning beneath him and her blood scorched a path into his stomach. His Cleo. She would be his. She would belong to him as passionately as he wanted to devote himself to her. No one else would ever get the chance to harm her, or to even get close to her. He was hers. He was drinking her in and she would never leave him. Her fiery skin branded his fingers as he got to his feet, eager to devour more of her. Her blood would throb around his body for the rest of his life, urging him on.

He bit down on her waist, breaking the skin and was rewarded with a new surge of her.

She whimpered, and the pulse of blood abated to a lazy dribble.

Thomas blinked, stepping back. Wiping off his mouth with the side of his hand, he stumbled back across the mattress and leaned against the wall. Everything was blurry. He watched the world from beneath a lake that was slowly being drained. It dripped away. The colour and the sharp lines melted into a blur, taking him with it, leaving him hungrier than he'd ever felt in his life. His stomach growled loudly and twisted in pain. He needed something, something warm and filling to sate the hunger boiling inside him.

He closed his eyes. He was remembering, or maybe forgetting. An elastic band was snapping into place, like a drunken high leaving his system.

The man had left after knocking him down, he remembered that much. Perhaps he'd bitten his tongue when he hit the floor. Yes, that made sense. Biting his tongue was why he could taste blood inside his mouth.

Opening his eyes again, he looked over at the woman. She stared, unseeing. Her eyes were finally as dead as the rest of her. The last of the colour had left her, leaving her grey, diluted almost. Only the remnants of beauty still clung to her. A faded photograph of the woman she might once had been. Thomas turned away and perched on the clean edge of the mattress. She was just another victim, like he would be when the man returned.

To think: he didn't even know her name.

5

Pain radiated from Spencer's shoulder. He'd not been able to make the turn onto the stairs in time, crashing into the wall instead. He launched himself around the corner, swung around the banister, and jumped down the rest of the steps, landing silently. Tugging his shirt down, he slid his arm into the sleeve and checked he'd remembered to do up his fly in his haste to get downstairs.

They'd all heard it, he was sure of that. Some of the older people in the house had probably returned to their beds, those who had seen too much to care about something as mundane as an argument. The others were most likely staying away out of caution, but Spencer had recognised one of the voices. Or he was hoping he did, so that he had a reason to be there.

He crept through the shadows in the corridor. The voices were louder here and Spencer paused before the turning into the entrance hallway, staying just out of sight.

"I should kill you," the first voice came. "I should have taken that boy you're hiding and torn you both into pieces."

Spencer turned and pressed his chest to the wall, peeking out from behind the corner. He recognised both men instantly. August stood in the centre of the hallway, his arms crossed over his chest, looking thoroughly bored. His lips tightened and he took a deep breath through his nose, lifting his head. Despite the look of indifference at the situation, Spencer could see his gaze following William as the larger man prowled around the room.

William was one of those men that could inspire fear in anyone, even other vampires. His knuckles crunched and clicked as he flexed his fingers, stalking around August's back. He wasn't the biggest man, he wasn't even the tallest, but he had enough muscle to wield a decent amount of power, his fierce dark eyes could silence someone in an instant, and the legend of his turning was enough to make people stay out of his way. Where others scattered when he passed in the hallway and shrank under his gaze, August watched, unabashed and unafraid.

"Where is he? The new one?"

August didn't reply. If Spencer hadn't known better, he might have thought August was a statue.

"You think you can keep him from me, Caine?" William asked.

His slow, methodical steps echoed through the hallway. He kept a distance as if there were some sort of barrier he could not pass. Prowling the perimeter of the imaginary shield, he taunted.

"The moment that boy steps out, I will snap his neck. Then I'll be coming for you."

The corner of August's lip twitched in response. Spencer gritted his teeth. Why wasn't he moving or arguing his case? Was he hoping that William would run out of rage? August had said it himself: William had killed seventy guests and then his own bride the day of his turning. There was no chance a bit of shouting was going to calm him down.

Knowing that August knew William well enough didn't stop the nerves from creeping up Spencer's spine.

"I will pull out his insides and use them to string you up across the front of this house," William hissed, his lips pulling back into a snarl. "You will pay for the blood you have spilled."

Spencer wasn't sure whether to laugh. The threats William threw at August were examples of reasons August had always been amused by him. William was a master of slaughter, and his crimes had been in the papers more than once as vicious acts the police were hunting for information over. Not many vampires could pull off blind rage; that was what August had told him once. Most of them learned that they needed to stay quiet and mostly unnoticed to get by. Not William.

Tension prickled and itched up his arms. He wanted to reveal himself, to step in and support August, but he didn't dare move against William. While August held a certain amount of power within their group, Spencer knew he didn't have the sort of clout to stop William from tearing his head off just to have something to do with his hands. Maybe his presence would be enough to take the pressure off? If he could just distract William for long enough for August to make his move.

"What makes you think you are so much better than others, Caine?"

Silence replied, and even Spencer held his breath.

"ANSWER ME!"

William himself across the gap, tightening his fist and pulling back, ready to strike.

August followed the motion. His arms twitched and the smallest tug of a smile flickered on his lips. Spencer stared at his mentor. Why wasn't he defending himself? Spencer curled his fingers around the edge of the wall, ready to launch himself forwards.

There was no sound to the punch. No slap of skin, no crunch of bones. August's head whipped to the side and William surged forward with force, but no sound came. August turned, circling around, and as Spencer saw the smile on his face, he realised that William's fist had never reached its target.

William was off balance. In his fury, he'd put too much weight on one foot. His other arm flung out behind him and August grabbed it with deft precision. He wrenched the arm back and up by the wrist. Swiping out his foot, he knocked the larger man as easily as he would someone half his size. William careered down. His knees hit the floor with a thud. His elbow smacked down and broke his fall. August tugged back on William's arm, just enough to prevent his nose from breaking against the tile, and placed his foot across the back of his neck.

Spencer snorted.

"Yes, yes, you can come out, Spencer."

He froze, his eyes wide in surprise. Yes, the sound would have alerted him to someone, but to him? He could pick out scents he knew if he concentrated, but August did it as naturally as breathing. There was nothing for it. Spencer stepped out of the shadows and approached.

August gave William's arm another painful tug. William gritted his teeth, but didn't make a sound.

"You knew this would happen eventually, William."

Fixing his gaze on the tiles, William took a shaky breath.

"You killed her."

With a snort of annoyance, August released William's wrist and lifted his foot from the back of his neck, retreating a few paces.

"She killed herself."

He was back on his feet faster than Spencer could blink. His fists were tight veined wrecking balls, and Spencer hovered at the bottom of the stairs, waiting to pounce forward.

"She didn't want to die. You talk so much, but you never had that connection with her. You never lo…"

August's face contorted with fury and within two steps, his grasp found neck. His short nails dug into the flesh and the scent of blood seeped into the air.

"If you know what is good for you, you will stop talking right now."

His words barely came at a whisper and yet Spencer heard every one clearly.

"You weren't…"

"If you truly believe that just because I didn't run around screaming my love that I didn't feel it, you are as much the troll as you act," August hissed. "Are you so arrogant to believe that no one loved her like you did? That boy downstairs loved her just as powerfully, it's what the sire bond does."

"Exactly, and you weren't…"

"YES I WAS!" August roared.

Spencer felt every bone in his body tremble. He took a careful step back, more scared of August than he had ever been of William.

Spencer wasn't sure whether it was force or shock that made William stumble back when August released him. He smacked into the wall and braced himself against it, staring at the man before him. A man, it seemed, he had never fully known before then.

Watching from his position at the bottom of the steps, Spencer wasn't sure he'd ever known August either. In the five years since he'd been turned, August had been a confidant and a mentor, he'd been a friend and more. Yet he only realised now that he knew next to nothing about the man who knew everything about him. Maybe that was what made him so terrifying in that moment. He knew now just how much August had kept to himself. Apparently it didn't matter how close he was to someone, he could still murder them. They said the sire bond was all consuming, that the loyalty created in turning someone was unbreakable, which was why they didn't allow it here. Yet, August had seemed cold and determined when he spoke of killing Cleo. If he could do that to someone he was bonded with, what would he do to the rest of them if needed? Spencer shuddered.

"You… you made her?"

August laughed, though there was no amusement or joy to the sound. There was only bitterness and hatred.

"No," he spat. "Did you believe yourself special, William? That she fought to save you where she had no other?"

"She never told me…" William breathed.

"I was turned before we came here," August said evenly. "We agreed it was for the best."

"And the boy?"

August looked at the floor.

"Will become like the others here, never remembering. Charles made sure of that," August sneered.

Spencer blinked and leaned against the banister. He'd never really considered his sire. From the moment he'd been aware enough to understand what he was, August had explained that they didn't allow sire bonds to continue unbroken. They were dangerous. He'd assumed that he'd never been under the influence of the bond, that it had been severed before he had the chance to feel it. He remembered everything else, so why did he not remember that?

"He's here, then?"

"Enjoying his twilight," August answered.

Reaching into his pocket, August pulled out a scrap of fabric. William's gaze shot to it immediately. His nostrils flared and his eyes widened. Spencer focused on the smells of the rag and could pick out the scent of Cleo's blood, having been around her so long. He couldn't begin to imagine what the scent would do to someone bonded to her.

August threw the rag over, and Spencer caught it without looking.

"Once the sun sets, you need to find him," he ordered.

"How am I…"

"Scent, it's on there. It's no different from tracking pray."

Spencer lifted the rag and held it to his nose. Inhaling deeply, Cleo's scent filled his lungs, but underneath it, the scent of someone else, the recently turned man.

"Why aren't you going?"

August glanced at him and raised an eyebrow.

"Would you rather dispose of Cleo?"

"No."

"Then I will be busy," he said dully.

He could see it then, the effort it was taking for August to hold himself back. He'd never noticed it before. He'd always assumed that August was just naturally uptight, but he could see the muscles working, the tightness in his jaw that refused to loosen. Spencer wondered if perhaps he was scared of letting go, of what it would do to him. He nodded slowly, and twisted the rag in his fingers.

"You should get some sleep," August instructed after a moment. "Believe me, with a new one, you will need it."

Spencer glanced between them. The hairs on the back of his neck were stood on end. He didn't want to leave August alone with William, not while they were both consumed with their loss. Stepping forwards, he was brought to a halt by August's glare.

"Go," August said.

"But what about..." Spencer jerked his head in William's direction. William scoffed in return.

"Don't worry, boy," he growled. "I'll keep him safe."

Pain twisted through Spencer's gut and he glanced again at August. He nodded back towards the stairs.

"Go, Spencer," he repeated. "I can handle Will. You have more to worry about."

Though his stomach only twisted itself into a tighter knot at the dismissal, Spencer took one last look at Cleo's two sired vampires and fled back up the stairs.

6

"And where exactly have you been, Mr. Trent?"

His landlady stood on the front doorstep, a cigarette dripping from her fingers. Her unpainted nails were short and chipped, yellowing with tobacco stains. She brushed a lock of hair back from her face and gave him the grin that always made him feel self-conscious.

"Hi Jenna," Thomas muttered with a guilty smile, bowing his head away from her gaze.

"Come on, Tom," she cooed. "Been out with a nice girl?"

She planted her hand on the other side of the doorframe, blocking his entry as she looked him over. The clothes weren't his, so he could understand her interest. The jeans were a little too long, scrunching around his ankles, the shirt too baggy. Thomas took a step back down the steps away from her and smoothed out the front of the shirt, Usually, he could deal with her incessant questions. He could block out the acrid scent of sweat and smoke, plastered over with flowery perfume that was far too strong. He could even laugh at the raunchy jokes that made him blush, but not today.

Thomas gritted his teeth behind his forced smile. The memory of the woman in the basement room was too recent and too sore to pretend to be happy. He'd considered going to the police but he couldn't think of what he would tell them. He didn't remember how he got there. The man holding him had been blonde, tall, in his early thirties, but had never hurt him. He didn't know the man's name or the woman's. He didn't even know where he'd been kept or what the house looked like.

He'd walked for so long, groggy and confused, that by the time he had thought to remember these things, he couldn't remember which roads he'd taken. He had absolutely no evidence of a crime, not after the man had given him a new set of clothes to wear. And they had just let him go.

That wasn't even to mention that he had been told that he was turning into a vampire. Whoever the sick bastard was, he was, at least, clever. The police would probably lock him up in an institution instead of taking his word and searching for a killer he had no evidence of.

"Just been working," he said finally. "Internship is all hours these days."

"Well, you'll be a good doctor if they ever let you get some sleep."

Thomas gave her a gentle smile. She pulled her arm back and took another drag of the cigarette. Ash fell from the end and landed on her shirt. Swearing under her breath, she brushed the offending ash away, giving Thomas time to slip past her into the hallway. His nose wrinkled, the cloud of smoke burning in his nostrils. Was it him, or was it more pungent than usual? There was a nutty smell underneath the smoke as well. He shook it off, he was just being paranoid.

Climbing the stairs to the second floor, he dug around for his keys. As he pulled the set from his pocket, he stared at them in surprise. He'd not thought about it until now, but the man had been thoughtful enough to move his keys to the new clothes. He patted around his hips and even his wallet was in his back pocket, his phone in the other.

He let himself into the apartment and closed the door behind him, locking the deadbolt. This was insane. He was going insane. He was calling a murderer thoughtful. The fact he'd been let go was odd enough but why give him back his belongings? Why hadn't they just killed him? Why—if the woman had been the target—had he been taken at all?

He tossed his wallet, keys, and phone onto the table. Stripping off his clothes, he pulled out a black bin bag and threw the new clothes inside. He tossed the thing down next to the door. He didn't want anything to do with them.

His apartment looked exactly the way it had when he'd left. The half-finished cereal was still on the sideboard, the remains of the milk letting off a stench. Thomas gagged. He'd never known milk to smell so bad. It was sour and layered with the sweet, wet, smell of mould. It made him imagine sandwiches left in lunchboxes and jam with layers of grey and green fur.

Covering his nose with one hand, he tipped the contents down the sink and turned on the water. It wasn't like it had been baking hot these last few weeks. Two days should not have done that. He knew the man had said it was three, but that wasn't the point.

The stench lingered in the air even after the water had washed the sink clean. He grabbed the washing up liquid and squirted it around the basin, hoping that it would help clear the smell but the lemon scent was almost unbearable. He threw the bottle into the sink, stalking through to his bedroom. He needed to sleep. Everything would be better after some sleep.

Except, he couldn't sleep. The moment he sat down he was up again. The reek of sweat and skin touched everything. He stripped the bed and grabbed fresh sheets, but they stank of overly perfumed flowers and ripe limes. He flopped onto the unmade bed, glared at the light that still filtered through the curtains, listened to the grumble of traffic and pedestrians, and stared at the ceiling for an hour. His mind was too busy to consider sleep, despite being exhausted. He gave up, showered and dressed, and fled the apartment. Company would make things better. He'd been mostly alone for three days. He just needed someone to talk to.

He found his way to the coffee shop two blocks away on autopilot. He'd spent the last year visiting almost every day and without even thinking, he was outside the door. He'd wanted company and hers would be best. She would calm him, distract him maybe, and things would get better.

The coffee shop was almost empty, yet when Thomas stepped in he could feel a buzz of energy all around him. He moved towards the counter, worried that he was going to knock into people, but there was nobody at the tables. One woman sat in a comfortable seat by the window and two men occupied a table by the wall. That was it.

"Hey Tom."

He spun around. The only employee of the small coffee shop, Paige, leaned onto the counter, resting her chin on her palm. The braids that ran from her temples had missed some wispy tendrils of hair that brushed her temple as she moved. Warm, tanned skin glowed under the low hanging lamps and Thomas could feel warmth rising in his neck.

He blinked, and quickly stared at the counter.

"Hey."

"Usual?"

"Uhh, yeah," he stammered, looking away from her inquisitive gaze. "Yeah, go on then."

He turned away from her as she went about making his order. He'd known Paige for a while and yet he'd never felt that sudden flush before. She was pretty and funny but he'd decided long ago that his crush was just because he hadn't known anyone in the city and liked that she'd been nice to him. After that she'd just become Paige, who was pretty, intelligent, funny, and made a decent coffee in the vicinity of his apartment. Paige, who was also nice to chat to if he didn't have the morning paper. Paige, who now brought a blush to his cheeks.

It was displacement. They'd learned about that in medical school. When someone went through a traumatic ordeal, sometimes they displaced the emotions into something else. They distracted themselves by focusing on something innocent. Yes. That was it. She was still just Paige. Only, the more he thought about it, about her, he could feel the blood drumming in his ears and feel it pulsing through his arms and legs.

No, he needed to stop this.

Thomas took a seat at one of the small tables next to the counter. Drawing out his money, his brow pulled tight over his eyes. The coins felt odd in his fingers. They felt gritty and as he rubbed his thumb back and forth, the taste of metal hit the back of his throat. The smell of coffee and tea were everywhere, overpowering. He took another breath, hoping it would clear, but the harder he inhaled, the more tones he could taste. There was the strong and sour espresso, soft and sweet latte, cinnamon from the flavoured tea. Citrus, berries, and mint floated down from the boxes he knew from experience were rarely used. Running his hand briskly under his nose, Thomas snorted the air out and took a resigned breath in through his mouth.

It wasn't much better.

"Here you go, Tom." Paige's voice was as light as mint and as warm as cinnamon as she placed a mug down in front of him. "Just the way you like it."

Without being asked, she slid into the chair opposite him, scraping the legs against the tiled floor with a shriek that shuddered through him. Turning her body toward the door, she leaned back, draping her arms over the rests and crossing one leg over the other. Her foot tapped a steady rhythm, and Thomas was sure he could feel the way the movement pushed the air in his direction.

The hairs on his neck stood on end, his cheeks flushed. His neck was feeling so hot he might have burned it and saliva collected on his tongue. He swallowed and picked up the steaming mug.

He didn't doubt that Paige knew how to make his coffee by heart, she took his order often enough. White coffee, half a shot of hazelnut, though he paid for the full shot, obviously. However, when he lifted the mug toward him, his nose wrinkled in disgust. The mixture smelled far too sweet and much too overpowering. Some people liked their coffee strong, but not him. She knew that. There was no way she'd have used that much for him. He set the mug back on the table and looked out of the window.

"Have I missed much?" he asked to fill the buzz of silence.

"Not a lot," she shrugged, twisting the end of one of her

braids. "Though, there was an interesting news article this morning. Police think they have a serial killer."

Thomas looked at her much too fast. His eyes watered and swam as another of the crippling waves of nausea rushed from his stomach and up into his throat. He coughed and covered his mouth.

"You alright?"

He cleared his throat.

"Yeah, I'm alright. Just, felt a bit ill all of a sudden."

"You've gone white as a sheet," she said, leaning towards him. "If I didn't know any better, I'd swear you were the killer, the blood drained so fast."

Thomas coughed and chuckled nervously. No, he wasn't the killer, but he was pretty sure he knew who was. Paige giggled and shook her head anyway.

"Sorry, Paige," Thomas muttered. "I guess... I guess I haven't really gotten over this bug."

"I was wondering why you hadn't been to see me," she teased with a bright as sunshine smile. She leaned across the table, her movements fluid and easy. The back of her hand was burning hot as it pressed against his forehead. He flinched out of the way but he could still feel the heat, even with inches between their skin. His throat burned like he'd drank the coffee in one gulp.

"Wow, Tom, I don't think you're over it at all," she said, shaking her head and sending a waft of elderflower and honey right at him. "You're really clammy."

Picking up the coffee, she went back to the counter and instead took down a yellow box. She picked half a dozen teabags from the box and slid them into one of the bags she usually reserved for cookies and muffins. Holding them out over the counter, she waved the bag in front of his face.

"Here, go home, make one of these, teaspoon of honey, and go to bed!" she ordered with the firm voice of a scolding mother. "I won't take no for an answer."

Thomas gave her a weary smile and accepted the small bag.

"Thanks Paige," he muttered as he got up and slotted the chair underneath the table. "I'll see you tomorrow."

Paige waved him off as he stepped out of the coffee shop, his shoulders hunched up to his ears, feeling very sorry for himself. Only, as the clean air hit his nostrils, the breeze and the open space washing away the overwhelming scent of coffee and closeness, he felt like he'd never been sick a day in his life.

7

There was a calm comfort to the routine. The steady plod of actions calmed the nerves for what was to come. He'd done it before. He'd gone through the routine so many times that he was beginning to forget the names. Most of the time, he even enjoyed it. He knew each of the steps and the order they went in. He didn't need to think about each element, and this time not thinking was preferable.

It could have been left until later. *She* could have been left until later. She wasn't going anywhere and it would have made not following the new one more plausible if he had to do it at night. He'd considered it, but he couldn't face the idea of leaving her there. Instead, he went about getting ready.

Spencer had returned to his room. William had offered his help to dispose of Cleo but he had turned him away. This was something he wanted to do alone. He didn't want eyes prying for each flinch on his face or for each word that could be misinterpreted. Alone was better.

The door opened at the slightest touch, swinging in and

hitting the wall. He stood in the doorway, unflinching at the sight before him. It was just another vampire who'd broken the rules, that was all. He tapped the toe of his boot in a quick rhythm against the bare concrete floor. Just someone who had broken the rules.

He had broken the rules. He'd broken them too many times to count. He'd lied about his connection to Cleo, he'd protected her and he'd disposed of those who would incriminate them. And that was only the start of his disobedience. In his mind, breaking rules was akin to those philosophies about trees falling in forests. Rules were only truly broken if someone caught you and he hadn't been caught, but she had.

Gritting his teeth, August walked into the room and set to work.

The contraption was the first to come out, as always. He unscrewed the latch of each hook and let her mouth free. Her lips, after being stretched for so long, were slack and hung apart like some drooling dog. He hated dogs. Grasping her tongue between his thumb and forefinger, he slid the spike out, pulling against the muscle, and tossed the contraption aside. It would be bleached, disinfected, and returned to the other boxes of odd devices, ready for the next time.

There was always a next time, even though people knew what would happen. People were always stupid enough to think they wouldn't be caught, that they alone would be given reprieve. Not her. She'd known she would be caught and what would happen. He'd asked her if she wanted to tell him anything before he'd put it on. He'd begged her to explain, or even to beg him not to, just so that he knew she hadn't given up. She'd remained silent, pliable, and had never looked away from his eyes.

Keeping up the appearance of enjoyment had been easier with the boy here. Now, he couldn't look at her. She wasn't the same woman he knew. Her skin was grey, her eyes diluted and lifeless. Her body burned hotter than he had ever known but there was no warmth to her. None of the warmth he had loved.

Sliding his arm around her shoulders, he lifted her away from the floor and untied the rope from around her ankles. Her feet slipped from the knot and hit the floor with a wet slap. August took a breath and didn't cringe. He lay her down on the clean part of the mattress and swept her colourless hair away from her face and neck.

"This was my fault," he murmured, crouching next to her. "I should have acted. We'd been talking about it for so long, and I always wanted one more year. Just one more year to make sure everything was in place. I should have seen that the years were killing you."

Things had to change. They'd been living this way for too long, and in the end it wasn't living at all. Living required change and nothing had changed for them in decades. They had survived, sure, they had enjoyed themselves, but they hadn't lived. He wanted to live and perhaps Cleo had too, but living had been too far a cry from their current existence.

They called themselves predators but they had been chained, trained like dogs to do as they were told and punished when they went against the rules. Why should they listen to the orders and pacts of those who had no idea how the world worked? Time had changed them all and it was time their rules changed with them.

August got to his feet and stared down at her, pushing back the anger. Only when he was calm again did he retrieve the chainsaw.

Usually this was his favourite part. There was a calm accomplishment to breaking a body apart, knowing that they would never return. There were other ways to ensure it and he was sure some thought him more vicious than William for his choice of method, but he liked the absolute finality to it. Not to mention that it drove the police nuts when they found an arm and nothing else.

Cleo used to find his little rituals entertaining. She would come to him during the day and perch on the end of his bed, suggesting locations to leave fingers. She would curl up in his tired embrace and whisper suggestions as they came to her. She would collect the newspaper clippings and stick them all over his walls. He would never spread the type of instant panic that William's outbursts did, but she enjoyed his quiet rebellions.

He started up the chainsaw, wondering where she would like to be left.

The blood that hadn't drained, what little of it there was, splattered in all directions as he went to work. First it was the legs, severed at each joint. The ankles were easy. If you angled the chainsaw in the right direction the feet popped right off. Bone wasn't ever much of an issue for a chainsaw but he liked it when things were easier than expected.

He remembered the song where children counted down through their body. Of course, with this, there were a few more elements. Disposing of a body was more like neck, shoulders, elbows, hips, knees, and ankles. Far more than head, shoulders, knees, and toes. After the hips were done, thighs oozing blood and tissue onto the ruined mattress, he moved onto the arms, one severed only at the shoulder to be delivered, and one at each joint to join the rest of the *bits*.

For the most part, he found that he was able to keep his

feelings detached. He thought of other things. He repeated his mantra that it was just another vampire who had broken the rules. When he came to her neck, however, he wasn't able to keep the words coming. He stopped, turned off the chainsaw, and sat down on the side of the mattress.

He swept his finger down her neck. Most of the blood had dried to her skin, crumbling at the slightest pressure and flaking away. There was a cut just visible underneath and, with a little push against her flesh, blood oozed onto his skin. He leaned onto his knees and stared at the dark substance against his pale skin. A substance that kept them alive and in the end killed them all. He lifted his hand and his tongue swiped across them. It tasted... dusty. It didn't taste like her at all. That scent that was so inexplicably her was gone.

"How long until it fades?"

August brushed his thumb against his fingers, smearing the blood into his skin.

"I'm not sure," he said. "It could be gone by tomorrow, it could take a decade."

William stepped further into the room. Like Thomas, he avoided stepping in Cleo's blood. He circled around the edges, staying close to the wall until he could look down at her.

"I never reached a century with her," he mused.

August stared at her, taking slow breaths, trying to keep himself calm.

"I did."

William chuckled bitterly and sat down on the mattress next to him.

"She always said you were competitive."

"I didn't know she spoke about me."

He nodded and leaned forward onto his knees.

"Sometimes."

William watched him with a thoughtful expression. August wondered if it was difficult for him, knowing that he'd been lied to for so many years. He'd often been jealous of William's freedom to have a relationship with Cleo. He was infuriated that the younger man didn't have to hide their connection behind closed doors. Now, however, he wondered whether he'd had the better half of the deal. While it had been hidden, their relationship had been honest. At least, as far as he knew. Knowing Cleo the way he did, knowing the ease with which she lied and hid things, he wouldn't have been surprised if there was more he didn't know. At least if he didn't know it, he could keep trusting her, unlike William.

"What will happen to her?"

"Her head will be buried with the others, the rest of her will be disposed of."

"You bury all the heads together?" William asked.

Lifting his head, August grinned.

"Well, you know, if decapitating them doesn't actually kill us, at least they have someone to talk to."

William grinned. Then he chuckled. Soon, both of them were laughing. They coughed and wheezed, loud barrelling laughs that echoed within the small room. He wasn't sure what they were really laughing about, his comment hadn't been all that funny. He wondered, in between gasps for breath, if it was just something they'd both needed to let out. They had both spent most of their lives shackled by a connection to a woman who now lay in pieces next to them. If they couldn't laugh, they'd probably end up killing each other.

It wasn't like William hadn't tried already.

"She wanted this," August said as he got his breath back. "She came back here with the new one for a reason. She wouldn't let me get rid of him to save her."

It was as if William was seeing him for the first time. The look of pride in his eyes was one August had only seen when it came to killings. There was also a sadness there, maybe that he had not been the one to protect her in the past, or perhaps that she hadn't cared enough to hold on. Either way, he got to his feet.

"Yes, well, she lived longer than most."

Smearing his fingertip along the chainsaw, August nodded.

"Maybe when your time comes to go bat shit, you'll let me do the honours?" William asked with a beaming grin as he made his way back to the door.

He laughed and stood, grabbing the handle of the chainsaw and hauling it up.

"Oh, I expect you to string me up to a building by someone's entrails," August argued. "You promised."

William held up one finger.

"That I did."

He'd barely disappeared around the corner before August pulled the tug on the chainsaw and brought it spluttering into life. He knew where he'd put Cleo's arm. It would be perfect.

She would have loved it.

8

Spencer sucked the excess from his fingers. He rubbed his thumb across the corners of his lips and swiped it with his tongue. The tips of his fingers had become pink with the extra blood in his system. Rolling his shoulders and stretching out his neck, Spencer shifted his weight from foot to foot, urging the blood around his body as he pulled the switch knife from his back pocket.

He could have just left him. The police probably wouldn't have suspected anything other than a robbery gone wrong but for safety measures he crouched and dragged the blade across the man's neck, obscuring the marks his teeth had left in his skin. Placing the blade between his teeth, he casually licked the edge clean as he dug the man's wallet from his pocket. No one would be too suspicious, people died in this city every day, when they didn't just vanish entirely. Robberies were common place and it wouldn't surprise the authorities that some went wrong, especially when the man looked the way he did.

He'd had that look about him. A look that he thought

himself better than others. Those types were often the quickest to get offed. They fought back, they talked down to their muggers and refused to hand over their cash. They were stupid. Luckily for him, and those like him, it meant that they were also easy and oddly rewarding targets.

Pocketing the cash from the wallet and turning the phone this way and that, wondering if he'd be able to see the prints from typing in the passkey, Spencer ambled away from the scene, back to his pursuit. He'd been tracking the new kid, Thomas, for at least an hour and while he knew August was counting on him, he figured that taking a break to deal with his own hunger would be more productive in the long run. He didn't want to find the guy then be so distracted that he lost him again.

He wasn't sure why August had left him to deal with the new one. According to most of the others, Spencer was still considered half a baby himself. Then, when the lifespan was drastically lengthened, he could see why he might be considered a child. His tracking wasn't even that good, what if he didn't find him?

Following the scent out in the open was difficult. He was used to enclosed spaces, watching people in bars and dark clubs. He was used to hunting those he came across by chance and following fresh scents, not ones that were ten hours old. August had said that it was all the same in principle, that it only took a little more focus. Luckily, with a fresh feed, he was feeling much more attentive to the task at hand.

The apartment had been easy enough to find. There had been so much of Thomas's scent coming through the open window that it was like a neon sign above the door. After that had been a little more difficult. The café had been closed by the time he got there, the waitress just locking the window bars in place. He'd asked her if she'd seen Thomas and she'd said he'd come in earlier in the day, but went home sick. Despite the stench surrounding the man at the apartment building, Spencer knew he wasn't there. He'd walked for a while, returned to the café and followed from there. Now, here he was, stood in front of a bar, watching the man whose scent was on the scrap of rag in his pocket.

He was young, probably a little younger than Spencer had been when he died which surprised him. August and William had both been in their thirties when they were turned. Knowing now that Cleo had sired both of them, he had been starting to think she had a preference for slightly older men. From a guess, he would have put Cleo around thirty as well, which, given how long she'd been a vampire, was impressive. This guy didn't look much over twenty. Perhaps August had been right, Cleo didn't really care about who she turned, she'd just wanted to die.

Why she hadn't ran at a cheese wire and got it over with herself, he didn't know, and he wasn't about to ask August or William. He'd never known his own sire. The man was gone before he'd had any sort of emotional connection to him. He remembered that they'd been having fun, and the next thing he knew, he had woken up with what he liked to call the 'Deathover' and his sire was almost dead.

Pushing the door open, Spencer went straight to the bar and slid onto the seat next to the man he was sent to chaperone. It wasn't the sort of bar Spencer would have chosen at a time like this. Any bar that put a napkin down before the bottle was not good for hushed conversations about the mechanics of vampirism. However, the dive bars were across town, and while Spencer enjoyed them, there was also always the chance you'd have a bottle broken over your head at some point during the evening. Also, not what you needed when trying to convince a newly turned vampire not to run for the hills.

"Corona!" he called down to the barman, who waved and collected up a bottle.

Spencer paid with his newly discovered money and slid the lime down the neck of the bottle before taking a swig. The hairs on his arm stood on end and he could feel that prickle of anticipation when someone was watching, even though Thomas was still staring at his beer. Spencer looked around but everyone seemed to be enjoying their drinks and conversations. Perhaps it was paranoia, this was his first time looking after a new one after all.

"Don't look like you're enjoying your pint there, Thomas," he said with amusement.

He lifted his head, glancing over before groaning.

"Just don't have the stomach for it," Thomas complained quietly.

"Have you even tried it?"

Thomas stared forlornly at his pint of beer. He hadn't taken so much as a sip, the glass was still full and Spencer could smell his breath, clear of alcohol and still with a hint of the toothpaste he'd used before coming out. For a moment, Thomas was silent. His brow knitted above his clear hazelnut eyes and he scratched the shaggy brown hair away from his neck.

"How did you know my name's Thomas?" he asked.

Spencer grinned.

"August sent me."

"Who?"

Pointing his bottle of beer at the younger man, he rested his elbow against the bar.

"August," he repeated. "Tall, blond hair, murderous bastard with a rather sick sense of humour?"

The colour, what little of it was left, drained from Thomas's face. Spencer could see it, inch by inch, the way his skin became thinner, like there was nothing between it and bone.

"He sent you?"

"To check on you," he explained casually. "You don't know how many are lost because they don't believe what's happening and they get caught with no protection at sunrise. Admittedly, I don't know how many we lose either, but then, if you're feeling anything like I did a few years ago, I know what you're thinking. Can I call you Tom?"

Thomas spluttered, blinking rapidly as he tried to catch up. He swallowed twice without drinking anything and glanced over his shoulder, checking the people around them.

"I... I guess," he stammered. "Wait, no."

"Fine, Thomas."

Spencer drank another mouthful of his beer.

"No. I mean, no, you don't know what I'm feeling." He lowered his voice and leaned in. "I saw a woman killed."

"Mine was male. I guess you're right. It's completely different."

Thomas' face contorted in anger. Bracing himself against the bar, he shoved his stool backwards as he got to his feet. Spencer took a gentle grasp of his arm.

"Sit down," he ordered quietly.

"Why should I?"

Spencer glanced over his shoulder. There was someone watching them, he could feel it. At first he'd thought it was August, that perhaps he was checking up on him, but he knew it wasn't. He would have been able to pick August's scent out, even in a crowded bar. This feeling wasn't August; it was darker and didn't feel entirely, dare he say it, human. The heat of anger felt feral and predatory. Spencer shook it off and gave Thomas a wry grin.

"Would you rather the polite version or the not so polite version?"

"The *honest* one?"

"I could snap your neck before you made it three feet."

The younger man looked down at him. His eyes narrowed and his nostrils flared. Spencer shook his head and leaned closer.

"At least hear me out," he said. "You've been feeling like shit, right? Thirsty but then everything turns your stomach, smells drive you up the wall, everything's loud?"

Thomas nodded

"That's how it starts. It will get better. Just sit down and if you don't believe me at the end of the night, you can go on your merry way, and I'll... I'll hide out until August no longer wants to kill me for botching this."

Thomas pulled his stool towards him and lowered himself back onto it. He looked furtively around them and leaned closer to Spencer.

"How can you be so blasé about this? He already killed that woman."

Spencer shook his head. Letting out a deep sigh, he rested his chin on his palm and stared past the younger man. All around them people were going about their normal Friday night. Women in heels so high they'd be complaining within the hour were draped over men in business suits. They drank cocktails and high end beers, wine and shots of expensive liquors. Spencer wondered if these were the type of people Thomas had been friends with before his... well, his death.

Spencer had not been one of these people. He'd never even aspired to be one of these people. His sire had found him drunk in a dingy club, where sex and drug use in the bathrooms were about as common place as actually using them as bathrooms. He considered asking Thomas where Cleo had found him but thought better of it.

"I can't explain everything, but it wasn't his choice to do that."

"Yeah, right."

"Look, the point is you have to believe in what's happening to you, otherwise you'll be dead before the night is out."

"What, because I don't drink?"

"No, because I'll fucking rip your head off if you don't stop bugging me with self-pitying questions," he laughed. "I ain't used to doing this, alright. This is usually Aug's gig. I laze about, I have fun. August does the hard shit."

"What exactly are you meant to be doing?" he asked. He looked rather wary, which wasn't surprising after a death threat, but this time he at least stayed in his seat.

"Helping you come to terms with who you are."

"Because I'm turning into a vampire?" Thomas snorted.

"Turning? No, that's already done," Spencer grinned. "I'm here to teach you how to be good at it."

9

August placed his hand down on the desk. He gritted his teeth, the sharp points of his fangs digging into the inside of his bottom lip. The man across from him watched serenely, a note of humour behind his colourless eyes. Charles was waiting and August knew what he expected. He expected some kind of outburst, or show of hatred. Perhaps he, like others, assumed that he would leave after being asked to dispose of Cleo. While none of them knew that he had been Cleo's, it was common knowledge that they had arrived together, and had remained in the city so that they could stay together.

He lifted his hand from the desk, leaving two white fangs on the dark wood. Taking a step back, he clenched his hands behind his back and waited. He held back the anger that was expected of him. It was too soon. He needed to stay calm until he was ready.

"It is such a pity that she had to be so public," Charles said.

"I'm sorry?"

"Well, if she hadn't been so public about it, maybe you

could have killed off the child before he had turned. That is what you've done in the past, is it not?"

The papery skin on his face didn't move the way August assumed it once had as he smiled in calm amusement. He reached out and picked up each tooth, rolling them around in his pale palm. Closing his fingers, he shook them like dice, his smile broadening as they rattled and clacked against each other.

August watched his hand. If this was when two others would come in and wrestle him upside down to be bled, they would have a good fight on their hands. He remained silent.

"Now, August, no need to be so modest, we both know you've handled matters for a long time now."

"I didn't..."

"Let's not lie to each other. With Cleo passed, there is no need for your little secrets."

"I didn't know you knew, Charles."

Charles chuckled. His voice was throaty, soft, and unnerving. He was used to brute force, to people who were loud and brash with their anger. He was used to William and the young who let their emotions get the better of them far too often. Charles was always so calm and gently spoken, even though everyone knew he had been able to kill without a second thought. You didn't survive as long as Charles had without being very good at what you did. Though, that was before time and blood had taken the beauty once afforded to him. Now, August could not remember the last time Charles had taken a kill for himself. He wasn't even sure if the man still knew how. As long as August had been here, he'd only seen the man drink that which was offered him in patronage. Not that he needed all that much these days. As the decades passed, the hunger abated. The new were the greediest of them all.

He was much older than anyone else August knew of. Despite having had the face of someone in their early twenties, the years had taken a terrible toll. Charles now resembled a mixture of someone in their thirties and an old man. His skin had the appearance of being detached from his bones in places, where others it was perfectly set. It made August think that half his body had decided to age and had forgotten to tell the other half.

August had never known him to look normal, so to speak, but the last century since his and Cleo's arrival had only made things worse. Charles now ruled from his apartment on the top floor of the house. He didn't go out, he didn't make his own kills, he rarely saw others. It was pathetic. Perhaps if he'd continued on he would have stayed healthy for longer instead of becoming the half-man, half-corpse he was now. He relied on others for everything, mostly August, and August hated him for it.

"There was little point in telling you," he admitted idly. "You killed the new ones off before they were fully turned, therefore, no rules had been broken. I wouldn't be able to punish everyone who killed someone now, would I?"

The impish smile did not suit his face. August took another careful step away from the desk. He shook his head.

"And our arrangement remains in place. You know better than most that these rules are not enforced for mere amusement, August."

"Yes, I know. Though there has been no movement on the other end. It seems we have missed the stake, so to speak."

Charles chuckled and dropped the fangs into a patterned china dish in the centre of his desk. He waved his wrinkled, papery hand.

"Yes, the rules of this little game do fasten a rather tight collar around our necks, don't they," he mused, cheerful despite the implication of his words.

August didn't particularly see it as a game. If it were a game, he would like to declare victory and slaughter the other team like mongrels. No, he saw it as chains around them, preventing them from ever being what they were truly meant to be. He longed to break those chains. He would break them, but for now he remained silent, staring over the other man's head.

"I assume Cleo's punishment will not cause any further issues?" Charles asked.

"No."

"That is good to hear."

He paused for a moment, wondering if he should bring his thoughts to Charles. The man had never really intervened with the way he managed the house, but if their current conversation was anything to go by, he'd seen far more than August had ever imagined. He wondered if he'd seen more of his relationship with Spencer and the thought sent such a shudder of paranoia through him that he stepped forwards.

"William was distressed."

"As he would be, being severed from his sire bond after so long."

Charles fixed him with a particularly penetrating gaze. His irises had lost most of their colour, pin pricks of black pupils swimming alone in a white sea. A crack appeared along the corner of his lip as they spread into a smile too wide for the skin to manage. August's eyes widened, both from the crack in the man's skin and the implication of his words, but Charles seemed not to notice August's discomfort, nor the tear in his own flesh. He drummed his fingers against the desk and leaned back in his seat.

"Well, I am sure he will get by. Probably with another dozen bodies, no doubt."

August nodded. He felt empty and bare. He pulled at the inside of his cheek with his teeth. Charles waved him off.

"Go, get back to life."

"Yes, of course."

His hand was already on the door handle when Charles spoke again.

"And August, eat before the night is out. You look positively dead on your feet."

***

The night had a cool breeze carrying scents of every flavour. The air crackled and hummed, electrified with activity on the busy street. Every night was busy here. Tourists flooded the streets looking for entertainment and locals kept their businesses open late to accommodate them. The heat of the day had abated, yet revellers still wandered the streets in as little clothing as modesty would allow.

The excitement in the air always reminded August of the circuses of the nineteen-twenties, back when he and Cleo had still travelled almost continuously. In those days the circus had been something astounding, not to be missed. It saddened him to see the farce they had become. The most attention they received was for the rides. There was no spectacle to it, just a sad collection of motor homes and poorly constructed tents holding rigged amusements. The animals were gone, protected by animal charities. The freaks were absent in a haze of political correctness. Even the clowns were a rare feature now that so many people found them scary. It was pathetic and mostly boring. If only they knew the fear true horror could create they certainly wouldn't be scared of an idiot in a wig.

Back then, when he and Cleo had found the route of a circus, they would follow and attend at every city, making sure to leave a trail of bodies in their wake. He knew for a fact that two circuses they had frequented in the southern United States had disbanded, believing themselves to be cursed. Spiritual folk were fun to torment like that. If anyone had known that they had vampires on their trail they hadn't said it.

Spencer's scent was everywhere. At every doorway August could feel the comfortable familiarity of the younger man. Some of the scent was days old, nothing more than a hint in amongst many other flavours, but he recognised the fresh trail quickly, following it along the main streets and ducking through alleys. At one point he came across a man in an expensive suit hidden in a dark corner. His throat was slashed and his clothes muddy. August smiled. His boy was a fun one; he'd known that since he met him.

The scent was stronger from there onwards and it didn't take long before August could see the two young men sat in a bar, drinks in front of them. He pushed inside, holding the door open a moment longer than necessary, carrying in the breeze.

Thomas, the new one, stared at his drink, morose and confused. Spencer, trained as he was, twitched and sat up a little straighter. A flicker of a smile pulled at the young man's lips and as he lifted his drink he casually glanced back over his shoulder. His grin broadened.

August didn't want Spencer to think that he was checking up on him, that he didn't trust him to take care of the new one. That hadn't been his intention. He needed a distraction, just for a short while, and Charles' suggestion of feeding didn't sit well with him yet. He just needed something to awaken that predatory instinct.

He strolled through the bar, a slick smirk pulling his lips as he felt Spencer's gaze following him. Thomas was speaking, some drivel no doubt, but it was clear his companion was not listening.

He did enjoy having this effect.

He didn't need to look over his shoulder to know that Spencer was still watching. Sure enough, he heard him excuse himself. He pushed through the door into the back corridor that led towards the bathrooms and, just behind the door, he waited.

He pushed through the doorway moments later, and before he'd had the chance to look both ways down the corridor, August grabbed him by the wrist, pulling him forward. Spencer's back hit the wall with a satisfying slap.

"August," he greeted with a grin. "I wasn't…"

August's fingers buried into the short hair at the base of his skull and yanked his head back, cutting him off. He stepped closer, trapping him behind the door. Spencer's breath was hot and dripping in alcohol. His chest heaved, and even beneath the cologne, the clean and heady scent was undeniably familiar and intoxicating.

"Aug…" Spencer breathed.

He stepped closer, sliding his fingers from the younger man's hair and instead locked them around the back of his neck. Spencer accommodated him and leaned his head to the side as August buried his nose against his skin.

"You've killed," he murmured, his lips tracing the hot pulse of blood beneath the skin. "Tell me, is that all you did?"

Spencer took three rapid breaths. His fingers hooked into the belt loops in August's jeans, pulling him closer. He ground his hips forward, glorious friction and pressure drawing a low, growling moan from the younger man.

"Yes," he murmured after a moment.

Scraping his teeth against his jaw, August pulled Spencer's scent into his mouth. His tongue flooded with saliva at the mere thought, yet he drew back. Putting an ounce of space between them, he ground his palm against Spencer's groin, another beautiful growl resonating in the air.

He captured the growl with his lips, crushing himself to Spencer in a deep kiss that left the young man gasping for breath.

"Keep it that way," he ordered. "Once the new one is safe, find me."

He stepped back, and Spencer reached out the moment their contact was broken.

"August, you can't be serious," he said quickly, trying to pull him back. "You're gonna leave right now?"

August grinned.

"I'm giving you an incentive to do a good job, Spencer," he taunted. "In the meantime, I'm going to feed."

He pulled open the door, swinging himself around it and back into the bar.

"You're a dick, you know that?"

He chuckled as Spencer called after him, but didn't pause as he returned through the bar. Knowing that Spencer's fury would be waiting for him at the end of the night instead of more worries about Charles or memories of Cleo, he was ready to hunt.

10

Thomas had no idea why he had agreed to this. He wasn't even sure that he believed Spencer. Yet he had followed him to the club, allowing him to lead the way as, after a brief conversation with the bouncer, they skipped the queue. They walked into the dark thumping room and Thomas immediately reeled back.

His nose was on fire, flames scorching into the back of his throat and sending smoke swirling into his lungs. Scents hit him in a constant assault and before they'd even reached the bar, Thomas had covered both his nose and mouth with his hand, his eyes watering.

Spencer didn't seem to be having the same problem. He sauntered across to the bar as if he had never felt so relaxed, leaned up against it, and watched Thomas with an amused kind of pity.

"It'll get better," he assured him over the din. He turned away as if it were nothing and ordered them two beers Thomas had never heard of.

"Really?" Thomas demanded. "I can hardly breathe."

"Trust me," was all he said. Thomas grimaced behind his hand and decided that he didn't trust him, not one bit.

The deafening thump of the music wasn't quite as bad as the smell but he was sure he'd have a headache within the hour. Was it him, or had clubs never been this loud before? This club also hadn't lowered the lights quite as dark as normal. Thomas could see perfectly through the haze of dimmed lights and crushing bodies. Whichever club it was that Spencer had chosen for them, he didn't think he'd come here again.

"Here," Spencer announced, handing over one of the bottles of unfamiliar beer. "Take a swig of that and focus on the taste."

"How am I supposed to do that?"

"Just try."

Thomas shook his head and lifted the bottle. The beer didn't smell particularly appealing, yet as he drank one mouthful and then another he found that it was preferable to the mess of smells of the club. It was sweet, more so than the beers he usually drank. He tried to focus on the different tastes, imagining himself to be one of those pompous wine experts who deduced there were oaky tastes to their cabernet sauvignon, or something along the same ridiculous lines. There was something citric about it, sharp but refreshing. But it was also soft and balmy. Sure enough, the more he focused on the taste of the beer, the less the other tastes in his throat seemed to matter. Not that it did anything to help the gnawing hunger in his stomach. In fact, like the smell, the hunger felt worse now than it had been outside. He lifted the bottle to take another swig before Spencer placed his hand over the top, pushing it down away from his lips.

"Don't drink the whole thing, space it out."

He followed Spencer to a small raised section just off the dance floor. They claimed a couple of stools by the railing, placing their beers down. Sweat, sex, and perfume hit him in equal measure. While Spencer wasn't looking, he drank another mouthful of his citric beer.

"So, tell me something," Thomas said, leaning in towards his guide. "If all this is true, and I'm not saying it is, how come I was able to go out in the sun today? Was that all a myth?"

"No, that's true," Spencer answered, slinging his arm across the back of the stool and leaning in towards Thomas. "You are in what we call the 'twilight'. The transformation takes time and in that time you get the best of both worlds. By the time the sun rises you'll be one of us."

"So no more sun?"

"No more sun."

"Good thing I'm not a lifeguard," Thomas grumbled sarcastically.

He turned away from Spencer and stared across the dance floor, listening to the music. The beat thumped through him, vibrating against his skin, and yet he could hear the melody beneath. He could hear each note and the harder he listened for that tune, the less he could hear Spencer's laughter. Glancing at the older man again, he blinked in surprise and dug his finger into his ear as the symphony of sounds returned in a crash, deafening him.

Spencer sat up straight, gave a short laugh as he nodded, and turned towards him.

"What is it that you do?"

"I'm a medical intern."

Laughing harder than Thomas thought was polite, he drank

a small sip of his beer, but even then, he almost snorted it out as the laughter came again.

"What?"

"You need to quit," he said. "You won't be able to do that shit now."

"Why not?"

"Because you can hardly control your senses in a club. How do you think that'll go down when you're surrounded by blood and open wounds?"

The frown overtook his entire face. He'd worked for years to get to where he was now and now he had to give it all up? Spencer seemed to notice his dismay and leaned closer.

"Look, maybe in a year or two, but you need to acclimatise. There are some things that will repulse you for a while, but others will drive you to breaking point... and blood hits the hardest."

Thomas still didn't believe Spencer, nor the murderer, August, but if what they were saying was true, he couldn't imagine being around blood would lead to anything good.

"I'm pretty new in the scheme of things," Spencer continued. "But those first few months were torture and from what I've been told, I wasn't that bad. There are some who go off the rails completely. We're talking mass slaughter."

"How do they get away with that?" Thomas asked incredulously. "If there are all these murderers running about eating people, why don't the media get hold of it?"

Spencer looked across the dance floor for a moment. His head rocked back and forth, following the sway of the masses. He licked across his bottom lip and drew the flesh behind his teeth. It was only then that he realised just how sharp the man's canines looked. He'd not had much to do with dentistry in medical school but he knew that wasn't normal. Reaching up, he pressed his thumb to his tooth and found it sharper than he remembered.

"People like August are the reason we don't get caught," Spencer said finally. "He trained me like I'm training you. Ways to throw the police off, stuff like that. Keep your head and you'll get by."

"But you're telling me I have to quit my job. Isn't that suspicious?"

"Tell them it's stress or something. You're going travelling or spending time with a sick relative. There are a hundred reasons to take a sabbatical."

"You're a font of inspiration," Thomas sneered. Spencer just laughed.

"Look, that's all stuff to figure out later," he said. "Tonight you need to get that first kill in."

"What?" Thomas's voice cracked and he quickly reached for the beer. Spencer laid his hand over his wrist, steadying him.

"You need to kill. You need blood in your system to carry you through the day."

"Why does that mean I have to kill?"

Spencer looked at him like he was mad and Thomas found himself shrinking away. He looked out over the dance floor as Spencer watched him. It was nearing midnight already. How many hours did they have until sunrise? Five? Possibly six? This guy was telling him that he'd be a murderer within six hours. He wasn't ready. He wasn't even sure he believed him.

"You are joking, right?" Spencer asked. "How else would you do it?"

"Can't I just get enough and leave them?"

Spencer's eyebrows rose against his forehead, his eyes widening, but there was an amusement there.

"This ain't a teen flick, Tom," he claimed. "What do you think happens when you drain someone of half their blood and leave them in the street? They don't forget, they don't magically heal. They get a great fuck-off wound and they go straight to the police to tell them that some bastard bit them. Dead is safer for everyone."

"In those stories, the… the…" He still couldn't say the word. It sounded so ridiculous to even think about, let alone have a theoretical discussion on. "The people have the power to change their memories."

"Well, you ever psychically addle someone or move a table with your mind you let me know, alright?" Spencer laughed. He swigged his beer and indicated out into the crowd. "Humans aren't such a different species. August told me that it's not like we've changed into something new, it's that we've reverted to something old."

"And what is that?"

"Hunters. Predators. You don't get any fancy powers like they show in the movies. We just use what we have better. You think these people don't smell everything you do? They do. It's all there, they just don't process it. They don't use it."

"We don't use all of our brain power consciously," Thomas agreed reluctantly.

"That's the one. Never was good with the numbers or the biology."

Thomas nodded and took a tiny sip of his beer, holding it under his tongue, focusing on the taste. It was much easier to think when he wasn't picking out a hundred different smells. He swallowed.

"So you're going to teach me how to use more?"

"Exactly."

Thomas huffed. His cheeks were burning as he gazed

through the crowd. There were some pretty girls out there, but he'd never felt the tingle of lust from simply watching a girl dance like he did now. He remembered the flush when he'd seen Paige. This wasn't exactly the same. Watching the women on the dance floor inspired thoughts of sex, but with Paige there had been something protective in his desire. He remembered feeling something similar, perhaps recently, but he couldn't put his finger on when he'd felt it, nor who it had been for.

He sipped his beer, letting his gaze wander. A girl in a blue dress swayed underneath the flashing lights, her green eyes glinting with every turn of her head. His stomach growled loudly and Thomas looked away, more embarrassed than ever. He glanced back at the dance floor, but he had to search again. The girl with the green eyes was on the other side of the dance floor. When he wasn't properly focusing on her she was barely more than another body in the crush. Maybe he had to admit it, Spencer was telling the truth. Well, at least in part. He might as well play along.

"Alright," he finally said. "What do I have to do?"

Spencer grinned and rested his elbows on the railing separating them from the dance floor.

"Let's take this slow. First, you've got to find the one you want. The one who'll taste the best."

"How do you suggest I do that?" Thomas sneered. "Go around licking their necks?"

Spencer chuckled and looked back at him over his shoulder. His amusement only seemed to grow when he saw Thomas's sceptical expression.

"While that would be hilarious to watch, it's simpler than that," he explained. "You watch. Your senses will do the rest. When you find one who... God, how do I put this?"

He looked out across the club again, and Thomas watched his eyes move continually over the crowd, though he remained as still as a statue. Thomas thought he looked like a lion about to pounce. He was so still that Thomas was pretty sure he wasn't breathing. A flicker came at the corner of his lips and the vampire turned back to him.

"Combine the best steak of your life, and the greatest porno you've ever seen. That's the one."

Then, with that bizarre and confusing image in his head, even Thomas started laughing.

11

Spencer shifted on his stool again, leaning onto the railing and hoping that he'd be able to get control of himself before he had to move. He emptied his beer bottle, trying to think only of the crisp, cold liquid that washed over his tongue and coated the inside of his throat. He tried not to think of August, or the red head currently wiggling her hips to some cheesy nineties tune. He was supposed to be focusing on Thomas. He was supposed to be teaching him, but it was increasingly difficult when August kept popping into his head.

He was a dick, that was what it was.

August would have known that his presence at the bar would preoccupy him. He never understood why the older man had the power to make him forget about everything, but every time he showed up Spencer let everything else go.

Then there was that unnerving feeling that kept coming back to him. Someone was paying them a little too much attention. He could understand if August had sent someone to watch them, to make sure everything went alright, but why hadn't they revealed themselves? Spencer gnawed on the side of his thumb.

Thomas reappeared from the bathroom, positively gagging, and went straight to the bar. He downed half his beer as he walked to sit next to Spencer and the relief on his face was clear as day. He'd forgotten to warn him about bathrooms, especially public ones. Those holes were foul your first few weeks. Thomas pushed a new beer towards him and looked out over the crowd.

"No luck?" Spencer asked.

"I found one," he corrected. "Just needed a... a minute."

Spencer chuckled into the mouth of his bottle and took a generous swig, pushing August's scent to the back of his mind.

"I did warn you about the sex aspect."

Thomas didn't look amused by the reaction he'd had to finding someone he wanted. Spencer had found it got easier as time went on. It reminded him of being a teenager and seeing his first dirty magazine. Back then, seeing a girl—or guy—without their shirt had been enough to make him get hot under the collar, but as time went on he needed more. The same was true with the taste of someone appetising. The first time had been embarrassing as all hell. These days, he barely registered a reaction until he had their blood on his tongue.

"Come on then, who's the lucky one?"

The pale blush that crept across Thomas's cheeks sent a warm flush through the air. Not as warm as if he'd fed, mind.

"It's a guy," he murmured into his drink. Spencer grinned.

"Alright."

"But, you don't understand, I'm not..."

Spencer's eyes widened and he blinked innocently.

"Not hungry?" he asked casually. "Or not gay?"

"Not gay."

He waved him off dismissively.

"Has nothing to do with it."

"But you said about the porno."

"Only as a comparison to how it'll make you feel. It's the thrill of the chase, the excitement of a hunt. It doesn't automatically mean you want to sleep with them. Though sometimes…"

Thomas was somewhere between looking horrified and understanding. He stared across the dance floor where a tall and tanned wouldn't be out of place on a runway looking guy was laughing with some girls. Spencer's nostrils flared and he quickly shook it off to take another swig of beer. He didn't need to know why Thomas chose the guy, just that he had. For now.

"Okay, so the next step is getting them alone."

"But I'm not gay," Thomas repeated. "How do I get him out of here?"

Spencer frowned. Thomas did have a point. He wasn't exactly screaming confidence and perhaps it was a step too far to get him to use a great dollop of charm on the guy. Men like that were hard to convince. When they were hammered it was easier but also more dangerous. He resolved himself to tell Thomas about that part later, when he didn't have the first feed nerves.

"Alright. Meet me in the alley round back, ten minutes," he announced, getting to his feet.

"Are you going to…"

"Yeah, I'll teach you charm one-oh-one later."

***

The runway model's name was Paul, said with a strong French accent that Spencer tried and failed to replicate. He sounded like an idiot but his little attempt had made Paul chuckle and roll his eyes, and so the connection was made. After that it was shots at the bar and within a few minutes, the guy was laughing and explaining in broken English that he was on holiday with some friends, but he didn't know where they'd gone.

Paul couldn't have made it any easier if he tried. A suggestion that this wasn't the best club on the strip, another shot at the bar, and he was trailing after him out of the club and into an alley as Spencer offered to show him somewhere better.

Thomas, on the other hand, couldn't have looked any more nervous. If Spencer hadn't known better he would have thought the guy was a junky waiting for his dealer. He paced back and forth next to the wall and stopped like a rabbit caught in the headlights as they approached. His eyes were so wide that Spencer could see the white go all the way around the irises. He stared open mouthed.

"How did you…"

"Hey buddy, this is Paul," Spencer said as they neared. "Paul, this is my friend…"

Spencer cut himself off, placing his hand on the side of Paul's head and knocking him sideways into the wall. The dull crunch echoed off the brick and Paul slumped forwards onto his knees before falling face first onto the concrete. Spencer looked down at him with a bland smile.

"What did you do that for?"

"Because you look like you couldn't hold a teenage girl still," he said. "And aim is important."

Thomas stared down at the man between them and as the scent of blood wafted into the air he licked his lips. Spencer had been worried at first. Thomas had still been reluctant to believe what was happening to him, even with all the symptoms playing havoc on his senses. Now they were here though, Spencer could see Thomas coming around.

"So I…"

"Bite."

His lips parted and he tentatively licked the tips of his teeth, as if testing how sharp they were. Spencer shook his head and crouched next to the unconscious Paul. Sliding one hand under each arm, he dragged Paul to his knees and nodded for Thomas to get down to their level.

Checking over his shoulder to make sure nobody was watching, he coaxed Thomas forward. Admittedly, it was becoming more difficult to focus. A dribble of blood was soaking into Paul's hair, sending the taste into the air. Spencer was glad he'd stopped to feed earlier in the evening. Paul, the would have been model, did smell pretty damn good.

"Okay, so get real close," he said. "You'll be able to feel the best place to bite. It's a lot easier when it's your sexual preference. You can kiss their neck, or whatever, but we can skip that for now."

"So I just… bite?"

Spencer cocked his head to the side, pondering it for a short moment.

"Yeah."

He'd not thought about it in a long time. It was all instinct these days. It had been almost five years since he'd had this lesson, August holding the unconscious body for him.

"You wanna lock your jaw back to get a good angle."

Clicking his jaw back to show Thomas a pretty decent overbite, he then stretched his neck out, turning his head and taking a deep breath, holding it in. He didn't want to get overcome with the scent of blood, and it was becoming increasingly difficult with the guy's head wound oozing and trickling down towards his neck, right underneath Spencer's nose.

Thomas hesitated for a minute, getting close and then backing away again. He moved his lips up and down about an inch from the skin until Spencer huffed.

He drove forward with force, canines digging into the flesh. He was off, Spencer could tell immediately. There was a little blood, that sweet and tempting taste in the air, but not nearly enough to say he'd hit his mark. Thomas pulled back, groaning in annoyance and frustration, before going for it again. Spencer shifted his hold on Paul, wrapping one arm around his chest while he tipped the guy's head further to one side.

Thomas tried a third time. His bottom teeth dragged along the flesh, and in frustration, he bit down hard. When he came away, a chunk of Paul's flesh came with him. Spencer wasn't sure whether to laugh or retch at the sight of Thomas picking bits of Paul from his teeth.

The bite had, at least, done one thing right. Blood spurted and flowed from the wound. Spencer waved him on. Thomas latched his lips over the wound, his chest heaving as he breathed snorting breaths through his nose, sucking it down. His jaw moved almost constantly and it was only as slivers of flesh slipped out of the corner of his lips that Spencer realised Thomas was using his teeth, driving further and further into the man's neck.

His breathing grew heavier and he grasped Paul by the shoulders, pulling more and more flesh. Grimacing, Spencer placed his hand against Thomas's forehead and wrenched him from the body. Thomas spat a mouthful of blood-soaked sticky flesh onto the ground.

Panting gasps rattled through his clenched teeth and his eyes were wide. He had a hungry look that Spencer saw very rarely. All of the others he knew were older than him, had better control than he did. Thomas was young and hadn't sated the thirst he had awakened. Spencer dropped Paul to the floor and leapt to his feet, grabbing Thomas by the arms and hauling him backwards.

"You're done," he ordered sternly in the same way August had done for him when he still tried to drag blood from an empty body.

"Did I… was it right?"

Well, at least he still had some of his sense.

Spencer glanced over his shoulder, down at the torn mess that had once been Paul's neck.

"Well, uh…" he grimaced. "You know, if anyone asks, we'll say zombies did it."

He gave him a cheeky grin and, for a moment, Spencer wasn't sure whether Thomas was going to laugh or launch himself at him in an attempt to get another hit of blood. Thomas snorted, breathed heavily, and finally grinned.

"You're right, you know," he said, letting out a short, loud laugh. "Best feeling ever. Can I do another?"

Spencer turned him away from the body and began leading him away down the alleyway.

"We need to get back. It's getting light. We'll continue the zombie apocalypse tomorrow."

12

August rolled over onto his back and blinked away the aftermath of lust. Slivers of sunlight wormed their way past the tops of the curtains where motes of dust played against the mottled ceiling. He dropped his arm over his eyes, relishing the black as a teasing hand slid across his abdomen.

There were still half a dozen daylight hours left but he knew he wouldn't get that much sleep. He never did. There would be things to do and people who needed arguments sorted out, the children that they were. Putting so many predatory people in the same place always caused friction and he was seen as a commanding figure, funnily, far more than Charles. Charles hid himself away, letting others deal with the problems. The old man hardly realised that his absence was slowly causing his inconsequence.

"I shouldn't have come."

"Excuse me?"

"After the way you left me in the bar, I should have got my own back."

August lifted his arm from over his eyes and curled it around his head instead. He turned to look at the younger man next to him and gave him a measured look.

"Spencer, what have I told you about bad habits?"

Spencer propped himself up on his elbow and looked down at him. His dark hair was mussed but his hazel eyes were wide and alert. He stared down at him, considering his answer, before shaking his head.

"That they hold no power over me," he sighed.

August took hold of Spencer's chin. He turned the younger man's head this way and that, mocking his admission, and pulled him down towards him.

"Right. Well, that's true, except for me," he whispered, capturing his lips in a quick, breathless kiss.

When Spencer lifted himself up again, his eyebrow was raised, nostrils flared.

"You're not a bad habit?"

"No, I'm certainly that, but I, unlike the others, *do* hold power over you."

Spencer snorted and August winced as the younger man pressed his finger roughly against a bite mark on his hip. His eyes narrowed and Spencer grinned triumphantly. He smeared the remnants of warm blood against August's cool skin.

"I make my own decisions."

August rolled his eyes and turned his gaze back to the ceiling, ignoring the tantalising scent of blood not quite his own.

"Of course you do, Spence," he murmured. "You chose to come here instead of finding some toy to kill after you played with them."

"You told me to look after Thomas," Spencer argued. "By the time he'd fed it was almost light. You're a convenience."

The way Spencer said it, August assumed that the younger man was trying to belittle the whole thing, like the reason he ended up in August's bed more often than not was because he was simply there. He chuckled and shook his head, grasping Spencer's wrist and guiding his hand down towards his hips.

He knew that it was more than that. There was no promise of devotion or obedience between them, but he was sure that in the five short years since he'd been turned the younger vampire would do practically anything he asked. Should he choose to claim Spencer as his own, he doubted anyone, Spencer included, would question it.

Nobody really claimed anyone anymore. When he'd been turned claiming someone had been the thing to do, though that was in the day when society loved its rules and proper place for everyone. These days everybody was so up in arms about equal rights and independence. Yet, when August gave the order, they still obeyed. He'd made it that way. He'd spent almost eighty years making it that way.

"So, how is our new one?" August asked finally, turning to look back at Spencer.

"Nervous."

Spencer licked his bottom lip as August took a sharp inhale of air. There was something to be said for the young. Sometimes they were stupid but they were certainly eager and had energy to burn.

"I should remind you of how you were those first few weeks," he chuckled once he'd regained his breath. "So tentative, so cautious."

Spencer's ministrations became confident and strong, as if just to prove him wrong.

"What can I say? I had a good teacher to get me out of it."

Adjusting his position, Spencer leaned over him and buried

his face into the crook of August's neck. August hissed as fangs pieced his flesh and the scent of fresh blood hit the air again, but the shortness of breath had nothing to do with pain.

There were those who revered his sire brother, William. Those who believed that his wrath and strength made him unstoppable, someone to be watched and almost worshipped. While August found William amusing at times, he was glad that he was not that kind of man. He was glad that he had chosen people like Spencer instead. Spencer, who was as vicious as the next when he needed but who was also charming and intelligent. His humour made him a magnet for prey and his sated temper made him easier to deal with than short fuses like William. August was careful in his choices and Spencer was certainly the one he was most proud of. Even Cleo had been impressed and kept the young vampire close when he was new. Though she had never admitted it to him, he hadn't needed her to, he knew that she liked his choice.

August considered himself lucky in that respect. He'd been born in such a puritanical time, a period where his desires had not only been considered shameful, they'd been illegal. There had been women over the years and there had always been Cleo, but he'd survived long enough to see the opinions on sexuality change. Spencer had told him the story of his own coming out but he knew the younger man didn't remember that conversation in the haze of his turning. He'd been waiting for him to reveal it again, to trust him with the tale of how he came to live in the hole he'd been found in. Yet each year went by and the man Spencer Allaway had been before his turning was fading away, making the story less relevant with each passing day. For how interesting Spencer had been to him back then, it was nothing compared to how he fascinated him now.

"Why are you not teaching him?"

Spencer stilled his hand, and August was caught between frustration and relief. He watched the younger man with a measured expression.

"Because I have asked you."

"But why?"

He let out an impatient huff.

"Spencer, I trained most of those here, and you know better than most that I am sought out constantly to deal with problems. I do not have the time or the inclination to train yet another."

"But he's like your brother, isn't he?"

"And you think that makes me want to be close to him? Cleo is dead because of him."

"But you said…"

"Spencer," he hissed, cutting him off.

The younger man's eyes narrowed and he drew his bottom lip behind sharp teeth. He didn't look convinced. August knew that if he really got it in his head that something suspicious was going on he wouldn't let it go. Grasping Spencer's wrists, he flipped him back with surprising speed, pinning him against the mattress.

"Would you rather I devote my energies to training a new one? Or to enjoying you?" he asked, raising an eyebrow.

Spencer's expression melted from suspicion to amusement. He lifted his hips from the bed and grinned, making no effort to free himself from August's grasp. In fact, he seemed quite pleased with the position he found himself in.

"When you put it like that, kill the new kid," he laughed.

"Let's perhaps not go that far, but now you mention it…"

"He doesn't swing that way, Aug," Spencer said quickly.

"You should have seen him when he realised he wanted to kill a guy."

Manoeuvring both of Spencer's wrists into one hand, August grasped his chin and tilted the young man's head so that he met his gaze properly.

"No," he murmured with a vicious smirk. "I have no intention of sharing you with that boy."

"Then…"

August leaned down, his teeth scraping against the side of Spencer's neck. He didn't pierce the skin, not yet, but he could feel his captive's breath quicken. How amusing that the same action could bring identical physical reactions from a kill and a lover. Spencer's breath came in pants of arousal where a kill's heart sped in fear. They both flushed but for completely different reasons.

Unable to resist, he pressed down harder, teeth sinking in just enough to get a taste. Spencer twisted beneath him as he moved to his ear.

"When you choose your next kill, bring them here," he murmured. "I might not want to share you, but I wouldn't mind sharing with you."

Spencer grinned broadly and with a gasp, August captured him in another bruising kiss. He wasn't going to get any sleep today, but with this specific problem to keep him awake, he found that he didn't much mind.

13

The mattress was hard and springy, nothing like his own. His own bed was soft and his toes often hung over the end. The smell wasn't the same either. While his sheets generally had the indistinct scent of chemical washing powder, these smelled of skin, sex, and apples. Green apples to be precise. He didn't know why he knew that. He just did.

Thomas's eyes opened much quicker than was normal after sleeping so well and he pushed himself up. A thin sheet slid down his side and crumbled at his hip. Looking down he breathed a sigh of relief that he was, at least, still wearing his boxers.

He swung his legs over the side of the bed, placing his feet on the cool, wooden floor. The curtains were thick and heavy and the room was still dark, but he could feel the itch of heat against his skin like he was already standing in the sun. The room was too stuffy. Thomas pushed himself up and padded to the window.

He'd barely opened the curtains an inch before he flinched

back, hissing in pain. A shaft of light, so brilliantly bright it made his eyes water had landed across his arm. He shoved the curtain closed, grasping the ends together and looked down. A pink strip of flesh, like the beginning of sunburn, glowed with heat across the inside of his forearm. Thomas grimaced and rubbed it vigorously but it didn't go away.

There were two doors out of the room and upon opening the first he found a bathroom. It was almost black inside. He blinked rapidly, his eyes adjusting to the darkness.

"Close the door," a voice groaned.

Thomas jumped and grasped the handle tighter. He glanced over his shoulder at the bedroom and slowly stepped forward, closing the door behind him, leaving the last remnants of light outside.

Through the dark, he could see the outlines of the toilet and sink. To his right, a large bathtub stood against the wall and Thomas frowned when he realised that there was someone in it. He blinked a few more times and, upon closer inspection, realised that not only was there a person in the bathtub, but they had a pillow and blanket as well.

"Spencer?" he asked.

"What?"

Thomas looked at the door before grasping the lid of the toilet. He put it down and carefully perched himself on the edge.

"Why are you sleeping in the bath?"

Spencer opened his eyes and the whites around his irises shone through the dark. He rubbed his hand over his face and shifted around, reaching up to punch his pillow.

"Too bright," he said. "Not to mention that my bed was occupied."

"I didn't hear you come in."

"Nah, you were pretty dead."

Thomas let out an unbidden chuckle, rubbing his hand over the patch of raw skin. Out of all the ways for Spencer to describe his sleeping habits, 'dead' was particularly amusing to him today.

"What you do to your arm?"

He looked at Spencer in surprise.

"How did you know?"

"Can smell it."

Looking down at his arm, Thomas realised that he could see it clearly. The darkness had lessened, like a fog clearing, and he could see everything in shades of grey and blue. The skin on his arm looked almost purple in the dark.

"I went to open the curtains and the light hit it," he explained.

"Rookie move," Spencer chuckled. "Give it half an hour and you'll be fine."

Spencer sat up, rubbing his hands vigorously over his face and threading his fingers into his hair.

"I thought vampires were meant to heal instantly?" Thomas asked, gazing at the patch of burned skin.

Reaching high above his head, Spencer leaned and stretched out his muscles. He rolled his head to stretch his neck and even shoved the blanket over the side of the bath onto the floor.

"Myth," he said. "And be glad it is."

"Why would I be glad it takes longer to heal?"

"Don't get me wrong, we heal much faster than normal people," he said. "But can you imagine if a broken arm healed instantly... before you'd had a chance to align the bone properly?"

Thomas grimaced.

"Exactly," Spencer confirmed. "Broke three fingers once. Was right in a couple of days."

Spencer clambered out of the bath and grabbed up the blanket he'd had over him. He wrenched open the door and grabbed up the pillow, striding through to the bedroom and dumping them on the end of the bed. Thomas stayed sitting on the toilet, the sudden brightness blurring his eyes, even though the curtains were still drawn. He could see now what Spencer had meant about it being too bright out there. Once he'd adjusted to it, he could see everything as perfectly as if all the lights were on.

"So, is this what you do?" Thomas asked. "Hunt at night and then sleep all day?"

Spencer tugged off his boxers without ceremony and tossed them into a laundry basket. Thomas stared at his knees, though he could see Spencer padding around, opening drawers and pulling out clothes. He tossed a shirt and pair of cotton trousers at Thomas's feet.

"Got a few days off," he explained, sliding a new pair of boxers up to his hips and tugging a dark blue t-shirt over his head. "Switched some shifts when I realised I'd be looking after you."

"Shifts? You mean… you have a job?"

Spencer leaned to the side so that he could look around the doorframe at him. He had a peculiar expression of amusement and incredulity, and he let out a laugh.

"Course I do. We all do. Well, most of us," he answered. "Get dressed."

Thomas grabbed the clothes at his feet and shook out the trousers to slip them on.

"Figure we can grab some of your stuff tonight," Spencer explained as he buttoned his fly.

"What do you do?" Thomas asked, ignoring the offer of fetching his own clothes. "I mean, how do you work if you can't go outside?"

Spencer laughed and nodded his head towards the other door.

"Come on, I'll show you."

***

Every window was covered with thick curtains or heavy blinds and yet there wasn't a single light turned on inside the large house. It seemed they didn't need it. As they descended a large staircase, Spencer explained that his eyesight would get better with time and soon he'd rarely notice that it wasn't daytime. The air conditioning had been turned up high, pumping a cool breeze through the house that did little to wash away the stuffy, hot air. Thomas covered his nose, which was once again burning with the different scents. Spencer said that would calm with time too. He was adjusting. That was the word he used, 'adjusting'. Thomas bit back the retort that coming to terms with being dead surely deserved a more dramatic phrase.

The house was spread over four floors, five if you counted the basement. Having spent time in the basement, Thomas wasn't entirely sure whether he wanted to count it or not. The second and third floors were bedrooms. A man named Charles had an apartment on the top floor but Thomas was not to go up there unless expressly invited. In fact, nobody went up there except for August and a few others who delivered blood on a regular-ish basis. That was another of Spencer's terms, 'regular-ish'. When Thomas asked how regular 'regular-ish' was, he said that he wasn't sure. Charles didn't need to feed as often because he was much older. August already only fed once a fortnight or so. For his first few months, Thomas would need to feed daily, or more appropriately, nightly. Thomas tried not to think about the fact that, within a few months he would have killed ninety people, depending on the month length. Ninety-one if you included the woman in the basement. He wasn't sure if he did include her.

Thomas flared his own nostrils as that rusted sweet tang of blood hit the back of his throat. He looked around them but nobody seemed to be injured. Even the burn on his arm had vanished. It was only as a teenager in an armchair lifted a mug to take a sip and left a pink stain on her lips that Thomas realised where the smell was coming from. The girl was drinking blood like some latte from a Starbucks horror movie. She wrapped her hands around the mug and held it against her chest, turning back to the laptop perched on her knees.

Five doors stood along the far wall and Spencer led him over to the first. He grasped the handle and, for a moment, stood and listened before he pushed the door open.

Inside, Thomas had to blink furiously as the light of a dozen computer monitors blinded him. Three people who looked to be in their mid-twenties had control of the monitors, each of which had at least nine windows of footage running.

"What is this?" Thomas asked.

"This is Tanner Security," Spencer explained in a whisper. "Officially, William owns it."

"William?"

"Oh, you'll meet him, but later. Later is better."

Thomas thought it best not to ask why it was better not to meet William until later. Especially since one of the men had turned around in his chair and was glaring at them both with an inordinate amount of hostility.

Spencer hustled Thomas from the room and closed the

door behind them as quickly as possible, without being considered cowardly.

"T.S runs the security for a number of office buildings around the city," he explained. "Those guys see something, they alert guards to attend the site."

"And each of these rooms has people watching screens?"

"God, no," Spencer said, leading him over to a large bay window and taking a seat on the cushions spread along the sill. Thomas could feel the heat of the nearby light but he took a seat next to him anyway.

"Tanner has the first, as you saw. The second and third are the tech branch of a call centre."

"What?" Thomas laughed. "You're kidding me?"

"Nope. They handle the engineering problems. All that 'have you tried turning it off and on again' crap." He glanced at Thomas and grinned. "Think about it, jobs where you don't have to go outside in the daytime, you don't have to go into an office, are really beneficial for us. We've got a couple people who work from their rooms. Heather is a writer. Apparently she's pretty popular. Get this, she writes Paranormal Romance… Vampires."

"Seriously?"

"Yeah. People love it," he explained with enthusiasm. "Can't get enough of that 'he could rip my head off but he loves me but he's just tortured' stuff."

Thomas raised an eyebrow as Spencer laughed. He was right. People had gone nuts for books and television shows about vampires, especially the teenage girls. It probably helped that they always cast brooding looking men with stomachs like oiled washboards. Thomas placed his hand over his own stomach protectively, feeling the slight squish of muscle that was definitely not toned enough to play a famous vampire.

Spencer, on the other hand, was toned enough, he'd seen that back in his room, but he didn't have the dark and tortured expression most people seemed to associate with vampires. In fact, he looked to quite enjoy his lot in life... or death. He still wasn't sure whether death truly came into the whole vampirism thing but he decided to keep that question for a time that wasn't confusing enough without theoretical discussions on life and death. He glanced at the doors again.

"What about the other two rooms?"

"Next to the porch you've got P.C.K, they design websites, and next to them is the room you do not go in unless the house is on fire."

"Why?"

"Because they design graphics on video games and they don't like being disturbed unless you're delivering them blood and Red Bull."

"Hopefully not together," Thomas suggested carefully, grimacing at the thought.

Spencer stared blankly ahead of him.

"You know... I never asked."

14

The second night with Thomas went a lot faster than the first. It was also much more enjoyable seeing as he didn't have to spend two hours tracking the guy and three hours convincing him that he was in fact a vampire. Thomas seemed much more at ease since this time he'd chosen a woman to bite. Spencer had to admit that he was surprised when Thomas had been perfectly charming with the woman and managed to get her outside. He had an easy, self-deprecating humour that she'd found endearing. Hell, Spencer figured he'd have found it attractive if it had been directed at him.

He'd made a mess again, pulling away far too much flesh. Spencer tried to show him how to get a clean puncture but he couldn't remember exactly how August had shown him when it had been his first kills. He didn't remember ever making that much of a mess of someone's neck but then again he didn't remember much of his first days at all. Nothing except August.

"So, how does it work?" Thomas asked, swilling his beer around the bottom of the bottle. "Turning?"

Spencer lifted his head to look at him. They still had a couple of hours until sunrise and, having both fed, they'd decided to head back to the house. Thomas, however, was still finding rooms stuffy and uncomfortable, so they'd retreated to the back garden, sprawled out on the grass with cold beers.

"Physiologically?" he asked. "No idea. And I ain't about to sign up to be the lab rat that helps them figure it out."

"Practically, I mean. How does someone do it?"

Spencer pushed himself up, leaning back on his hands as he surveyed Thomas thoughtfully.

"Well, first of all, you don't."

"I don't follow."

"We're not allowed," he explained. "There are very strict rules to living here. We all chip in with work and money, get blood if people can't get out for themselves, and we don't turn people."

"That doesn't make any sense. If you're not allowed to turn people, then why am I here?"

Spencer looked away from him, staring into the black shadows of the trees that lined the garden. He'd not considered having to be the one to explain all this to him. Explaining the practical lessons of how to feed was one thing, but he didn't think he was the best person to tell Thomas about Cleo.

"Sometimes people break the rules."

"And what happens?" Thomas asked casually.

"Do you remember much about turning?"

"There are gaps. That guy, August, said I'd been there three days, but I don't remember it being that long."

"You remember being with someone?"

"The woman, yes," Thomas answered. "She was there for me to drink, right? To complete the process."

Spencer shook his head.

"Her name was Cleo," he said quietly. "She was the one who turned you."

Thomas stared at his beer for a long time. Running his finger around the mouth of the bottle, he licked his lips and gulped.

"You knew her?" he asked finally, his voice no more than a breath of a whisper.

"We all did," Spencer said. "Cleo was one of the oldest of us. She…"

Spencer fell silent. He grabbed his beer from where he'd stood it in the grass and took a large gulp, focusing on the soft taste.

"She what?"

"She was like a mother, or a big sister, something like that, to a lot of us."

Thomas sat silently, his lips parted, his eyes staring at nothing. The taste of alcohol on his breath danced in the breeze. Spencer held his breath.

"And she was killed because of me?"

Spencer didn't want to lie to him. Thomas was a good guy and he hadn't done anything to deserve the blame being placed on him. Yes, he had lived whilst Cleo had been bled and killed but he had no choice in the matter. Nobody had even considered giving him a choice as far as Spencer knew. If he'd been given a decision with his own turning, he didn't remember it.

"No," he insisted. "She was killed because she broke the rules. Whether you'd turned or not, she wouldn't have lived."

Thomas gave a small glum nod, though Spencer wasn't entirely sure that Thomas believed what he was being told. He began picking at the label on his beer bottle, tearing it from the glass in thin strips that were discarded into the grass.

"Did I kill her?"

"I'm sorry?"

"This Cleo? Did I finish it? I remember that… I remember that she was alive the first time I woke up. She kept staring at me. Then, when *he* let me out, she was dead. Did she just bleed to death, or did I…"

"You drank her, yes," Spencer concluded. "It's the last stage of turning. First the vampire drinks you, then they feed you some of their blood. You lose some time as it begins to change you and then you need to drink more from them. If Cleo had been, let's say 'more aware', she would have stopped you before you killed her, but she had already lost too much blood. You finished it."

"So that's the way to kill a vampire? To drain their blood?"

"It's one of the ways, yes."

"What are the others, garlic? A stake through the heart? Holy water?"

Spencer laughed loudly. He didn't remember asking these questions himself, but seeing as he knew the answers, he figured that he must have done at some point. Maybe it had been the same for him. He remembered bits and pieces, like photographs of a particularly good day out. The bits in between, however, were blurry.

"You're not going to be hunted down by priests wielding garlic bread," he chuckled. "Though, I doubt you'll be eating it any time soon."

"Why? If it's not dangerous, why shouldn't I?"

"You ever eaten an entire head of garlic?"

Thomas glared at him, his eyes narrowed.

"No."

"You already know how much stronger your sense of smell

is and garlic is no different. It's not dangerous, but it isn't pleasant."

"So, I'm stuck with eating bland food the rest of my... I want to say 'life', but I'm not sure if that's right."

"Call it whatever you want," Spencer shrugged. "But not entirely. You just learn to be a lot more careful with seasoning. You can use the smallest pinch of chilli, and a meal is spicy, stuff like that."

Thomas paused to swig his beer and Spencer could see him swilling the liquid around in his mouth. His absent gaze was thoughtful. He was testing his taste buds.

"Alright, so what about the rest?" he asked once he'd swallowed.

"Well, you've had fun with sunlight already," Spencer replied. "Stake through the heart works but then that'd probably kill anyone if they didn't get to a hospital quick enough. Decapitation, burning. All the fun ways to die."

"You and I have very different ideas of fun."

Spencer finished off his beer and grinned.

"Just don't be an idiot and you won't have to worry about that stuff for a long time."

"Well, I don't know about that," a man said behind them.

They both jumped. Thomas was on his feet in an instant with a slightly surprised look on his face that had nothing to do with the man standing at the top of the steps. He glanced down at the flattened grass he'd been sitting on and shook his head as if pushing away a particularly niggling thought.

Spencer looked over his shoulder and tried to suppress a shudder.

"Hello, William."

William took each step slowly, his gaze never leaving Thomas. He raked over the man from head to foot, his lips pursed and his eyes narrowed. He cracked his knuckles.

"So, this is the boy."

Thomas took a tentative step backwards, holding the beer bottle against his stomach.

"Yes," Spencer replied. "This is Thomas. Tom, this is William."

"H…Hi William," Thomas murmured.

"This is the boy Cleo gave her life for."

It wasn't a question and Spencer could feel the waves of tension coming off William. Carefully he got to his feet, shoving his hands into his pockets. He moved to stand next to Thomas.

"It wasn't like that and you know it. August already…"

"August did what he was told like a good little lapdog," William growled. He grasped the wooden banister running down the steps and Thomas flinched beside him as the wood buckled and crunched under William's strong grasp.

Spencer held his ground, though he had no idea how far that would get him. He wanted to retreat like Thomas had. He'd seen William kill once, and once had been enough. Where most tried to make their kills look like robberies gone wrong, or even accidents, William practically ripped his victims apart. Spencer shuddered.

"August…"

William laughed.

"Always sticking up for August, aren't you boy," he said. "If I didn't know better…"

He stopped, a look passing through his eyes that on most might have simply looked thoughtful or inquisitive. On William, it looked predatory and downright terrifying. Spencer took a deep breath and gritted his teeth, the points of his fangs digging into his bottom lip as William came closer. Thomas lost all restraint and jumped back a few paces. William barely glanced at him, his attention now firmly fixed on Spencer.

William didn't try to move quickly. Spencer could see what was going to happen with enough time to avoid it but he balled his hands into fists and didn't fight back as William grasped his throat. There was no way he would win a physical fight against William. He wasn't as fast as August and he wasn't tactical. Not provoking him was the best he could hope for. William leaned close.

"You're close to him, aren't you?" he asked.

"I... I guess," Spencer breathed. William's grip tightened and it felt like his windpipe was being crushed back against his spine.

"Protective little bastard."

Spencer didn't know what to say to that, if he could say anything at all the way William's fingers crushed into his neck. He settled for failing to gulp, choking against William's hand. Blood rushed through him thanks to the recent feed, hammering against his skin. He could feel it throughout his body like he was vibrating to a fast baseline.

William laughed very suddenly and released him.

"That cheeky fucker!" he roared. "That sneaky, manipulative..."

Rubbing his neck, Spencer took a hasty step away from William. However, the larger man seemed to have completely lost interest in him and Thomas. He shook his head, crossing his arms over his chest and turned, stalking back up the steps and into the house without another word.

Spencer stood there, staring after William as Thomas returned to his side.

"Who is William?"

Spencer glanced at Thomas and instantly regretted it as his

neck seared in pain. He groaned under his breath and massaged the sore muscles.

"William is the other guy that Cleo turned," he said. "He's also the most vicious guy you'll ever meet."

"So stay away?" Thomas asked, coming to stand next to Spencer and staring up at the house.

He winced as he nodded.

"Stay away," he agreed. "Stay far, far away."

15

August slipped into his bedroom, hoping that his return to the house had gone unnoticed. He'd left the moment the sun had set. Some much needed time to himself was difficult to come by these days. Or it had been.

For the first time in a hundred and seventeen years he was alone inside his head.

The first time he'd felt it, or more appropriately hadn't felt it, had been early that morning. He'd felt Cleo's presence for over a century. It had become such a natural part of his life that he'd rarely considered the bond until it was gone. Although it wasn't gone completely yet, there were brief moments where it flickered and faded before flaring back into life.

He wasn't completely alone, there were still the others but the tethers he had created with them were weak, fluctuating with mood and proximity. Cleo had been constant. August sat on the corner of his bed and massaged his temples.

William didn't knock before opening the door. Light from the hallway flooded in but August didn't lift his head. He didn't have to. If he'd felt the loss of the connection then William must have too. Doubtless the younger vampire wanted to berate him about her death again.

"I had an interesting conversation with the boy," William muttered.

August sighed.

"Tormenting the new one won't bring her back, Will."

The door clicked closed. William stepped further into the room and out of the corner of his eye, August saw his hands propped on his hips.

"No, that one is quite pathetic from the looks of it," he said. "I meant your boy, August."

Lifting his head, August's eyes narrowed. He licked across his bottom lip.

"And what exactly is that supposed to mean?"

"I know what you're doing."

"Really?" August sneered. "That makes one of us."

William grasped the back of the chair from underneath the small desk against the wall. He swung it around easily and sat down, leaning forward until their eyes were level.

"It's funny how eager the boy is to protect you, August."

August rolled his eyes and looked away.

"I know words are not your forte," he growled. "But should you choose to explain what the hell you are talking about any time soon..."

"Spencer," he hissed in return. "I know what you've done to him. You kill others who break the rules, but you're above them yourself?"

Sitting up straight, August stared back at him, an unease settling in his stomach. It was a guess, nothing more.

William had been turned straight into this group. He did not know enough to know for sure.

"There are no rules on who I take into my bed, William. Whether I choose Spencer or someone else is no business of yours."

"But who you sire," William said, "I believe, is everyone's business."

August's flinched and grasped the duvet beside his legs.

"I've done no such thing. Ask him if you want. He remembers his sire enough to tell you it wasn't me."

William laughed and edged the chair closer.

"Oh, I have no doubt that the vampire who turned him was punished accordingly. By you no doubt."

"Are you aware of some form of siring that I am not, William?" August demanded, his voice rising, reaching close to breaking point. "Spencer was turned, his sire was killed. I have no idea what you're talking about."

"Don't play dumb with me, August," William snapped. "You do not do it nearly as well as I do."

August gritted his teeth and pushed himself further away from the bigger man. He didn't like where this was going. Nor did he like the flare of anger in the man's narrowed eyes, the way his fingers dug into his own flesh as if desperate for something more violent to grip onto.

"You may not have turned the boy but you are his sire."

"You don't know what you're talking about," August rasped.

He got to his feet, walking quickly across the room to put some space between them. This was insane. His connection to Spencer was the strongest it had ever been and yet right now he wanted him out of his head, even if only for a short while. He wanted to have his mind to himself while he grieved. He knew it wouldn't happen but even the thought of losing him turned his stomach.

"Does the boy even realise that his preference for you is not of his own making?"

"It's not like that," August breathed.

Behind him, William chuckled.

"Is he the only one?"

He spun to face the younger man.

"How did you know?"

William leaned away from him and August let out a breath of relief. However much he tried to deny it, William sometimes made him nervous. The idea that he knew what August had been doing made it all the worse.

Not that what he'd been doing was technically against their laws. The law was that you weren't allowed to turn anyone without permission, not that you couldn't sire them. However, they'd passed the rule off as protecting their group from the split loyalties that sire bonds created. They'd lied for almost a century and those who didn't know the truth would certainly see his connection to Spencer as a breach.

"I told you, he is too eager to protect you. I doubt he feels it as strongly as if he would had you been the one to turn him but there is a connection there."

August nodded.

"Is he the only one?" William repeated.

Watching William for a moment, he wondered if he could get away with the lie. It would be safer to lie. If William chose to seek his vengeance by taking Spencer, at least the others would be safe.

August gulped. He couldn't sacrifice Spencer.

"No," he answered in a whisper. "He's not. There are six others."

This time, it was William's turn to be surprised. He stared at the wall past him, chewing on the inside of his cheek.

"You've been busy," he said finally.

"No, not busy. Just methodical."

"And they were all turned by others?"

August nodded.

"I knew that I would never get away with turning someone myself, so I... made arrangements."

"They were chosen before they were turned?" William asked.

Rubbing his hand over his face and around the back of his neck, August stared at the door.

"Only Spence," he murmured. "I lost one in order to turn him."

"How long has this been going on?"

"Longer than you've been doing what you do to keep busy," he said. "The first was an accident. I didn't even realise what was happening until Cleo pointed out the loyalty they had to me. After that it became a habit."

This, at least, he could be proud of. William had been blissfully unaware of how long he had been operating under everyone's noses. While others were disposed of to sever the sire bonds, he had been careful to create them. He did it slowly, in a way that could go undetected. It was only the stronger bond to Spencer that had led William to his discovery. He wondered whether he should distance himself from the younger man for a while to disperse any suspicions but even as he thought it, a hole opened up in his stomach. He was already feeling Cleo's absence, he wasn't sure he could suffer Spencer's as well.

113

"Cleo knew?"

August grinned.

"She chose a few of them," he answered. "She chose you."

He watched realisation dawn on William's face. He met his gaze, a mischievous smirk greeted a surprised frown.

"I was a part of this?"

"Finding someone to turn you proved... difficult. With your wedding coming, she was worried about missing our chance, so she turned you herself."

William continued to stare at him, his lips parted, his fingers digging into his knees.

The shrill ring shocked them both from their silence. William's gaze snapped away from him and found the offending device. It rang again. August went to the bed and collected it from the pillow, turning it over and staring down at the name lit up on the screen. For a moment he considered denying the call, letting it go to voicemail, but one look at William's face told him that wasn't a good idea. Seeing his caution, William waved him on.

August swiped open the phone.

"What is it, Spencer?"

Across from him, William snorted, his concern about his turning forgotten.

"It's Thomas," Spencer said, his voice cracking. "There's a problem."

August went to the window and twitched open one of the curtains. A white gold dawn was fast approaching. He swept the curtain shut against the oncoming light.

"Where are you? You should be back by now."

"I can't!" Spencer hissed. He was trying to be quiet but August couldn't work out why. There was no music or heavy beat from a club in the background. He couldn't hear anyone else speaking so he wasn't at a party or with friends. The hairs on August's neck were standing on end as he twitched the curtain again.

"Why not? If you run, you'll make it."

August didn't like the panic in Spencer's voice. He could hear the drum of constant footsteps, the squeak of soles on a tiled floor.

"I'm trapped in a coffee shop. Thomas won't move."

"What do you mean, won't?"

Spencer's breath crackled down the phone. August could hear a woman hammering on a door in the background, asking someone to come out. She sounded even more terrified than Spencer did.

"He fed on a junkie," Spencer admitted finally. "He's tripping."

"What?" August growled. He glanced at William, who was listening in with amused interest. "How could you be so stupid?"

He'd taught Spencer well when he was first turned. He'd seen possibilities in him that he'd not found in a long time and he'd taken his training on himself despite the risk of being discovered. Feeding off junkies was dangerous. It was incredibly fun if done right and August had enjoyed the amplified high more than once but he'd taught Spencer to be cautious. If you took the wrong drug the effects could be disastrous when it was enhanced in the passing from bloodstream to bloodstream.

"That's not the worst part…"

August took a deep breath and rubbed his hand over his face. He didn't know how much more bad news he could take. Despite the quiet of Cleo's absence in his head, his thoughts were more crowded than ever.

"What is the worst part, Spencer?"

"He… he got the munchies," Spencer breathed, his voice coming painfully quiet, scared. "August…"

There was a breath and he heard Spencer gulp.

"August, there's been a massacre."

16

The squeak of rubber against the tiled floor vibrated in Spencer's ears distracting him. He paused, staring at a blank patch of wall before he began moving again. Perhaps distraction was good. It had to be better than waiting. When he reached the door he edged one of the blinds up, careful to keep his hand out of the path of sunlight. Only, none came. He lowered his head and glanced through the gap. Dawn was fast approaching but had not yet arrived. There was still time.

It was a nice coffee shop, one of those cool little independent places that had bookshelves crammed with paperbacks, comfy chairs, and didn't kick you out the moment you finished your drink. The chairs didn't match and the tables were scratched to hell but the drinks were cheap and delicious and the food was handmade. It was the kind of place he would have hung out back before he'd been turned. Well, if he could have afforded it, he would have hung out there.

Spencer glanced over at the woman. She hammered on the bathroom door again, calling out to Thomas. Her hair was dishevelled and her tanned skin had lost any glow it usually held. She glanced over her shoulder at him.

"Aren't you going to do something?" she demanded.

"Like what?"

"Get him out of there? Call the police? Anything!"

Spencer shook his head and went back to his pacing.

"You don't want me to get him out of there," he said. "And no, I'm not calling the police. He will be here to sort this out."

"Who?"

Glancing over his shoulder, he saw the look of panic on her face. He gritted his teeth and looked away from her. The scent of blood had consumed everything in the small coffee shop and his hunger was clouding his senses. The woman smelled good... too good. It was becoming distracting and not the kind of distraction he wanted. It was the kind of thing he was trying to keep himself distracted from.

Spencer froze at the sound, a subtle click and then the chiming of artificial bells. He spun on his heel, leaping across the shop. He wrapped one arm around her waist, pulling her back against his chest and snatched at the phone in her hand.

"I said no!" he snarled.

"I don't care!" she cried back, frantically trying to hit the numbers while keeping the phone from his reach. "He killed people!"

Spencer grasped the phone and pried it from her fingers. Her sob shuddered through him, and after pocketing the device, he dragged her over to a comfy looking chair.

"I'm sorry," he murmured, guiding her into the cushions. "This is horrifying for you, I get that."

"How is it not horrifying for you?"

Spencer reached out and carefully tucked a lock of hair

behind her ear. She flinched but didn't pull away.

"He was telling the truth."

"Oh, don't be ridiculous," she snapped, batting his hand away. "He's been too stressed with his internship. He snapped, you know, mentally. He's not…"

"Do you know how difficult it is to bite through someone's neck deep enough to get blood?"

The woman froze and stared up at him, her eyes wide.

"You saw what he did," Spencer insisted. "He didn't use a knife. He didn't shoot those people. He tore through seven necks in less than a minute."

"And you're…"

"The same."

She stared at her thighs. Her fingers curling around her knees and digging in tight as she pulled her legs up to her chest. Her face had a vacant look to it and Spencer sat down on the corner of a worn coffee table, watching her. Thomas had locked himself in the back room with the bodies. He was probably taking too much from them but there was nothing he could do for him right now. No, he couldn't help the young vampire, but he could make sure this woman didn't call the police or go running into the street to tell everyone she could find that there was a vampire massacre going on in a dinky little coffee shop.

"Paige!" she cried suddenly.

"What?"

She reached out and grasped his hands, pulling him closer.

"My name is Paige. I'm twenty-four. I've worked here for three years but I make stuff. Jewellery, hair clips, little sculptures. I like metal work mostly. I have a brother, he's sixteen. Lives with my parents and they'd miss me. They'd all miss me."

"What?" he demanded in confusion. "Why are you telling me this?"

"They say a murderer is less likely to kill you if they know things about you," she babbled. "That they'll remember you're a person and it makes it more difficult."

Spencer gave a small laugh and glanced over his shoulder. He was sure that he'd heard something.

"Don't worry, Paige," he smiled. "Not gonna kill you. Even if I was I think it's too late. He's here."

Despite Paige's protests at having more "vampires"—a word she quoted with her fingers—inside the coffee shop, she handed over the keys to the door and didn't argue as Spencer unlocked it and slid open the deadbolt. He stepped behind the door as he pulled it open, shielding himself in case the sun had decided to show its face. Two car doors snapped, one after the other, and two masked, hooded, and heavily dressed men sped past him. Spencer closed the door and locked it. He looked at the two men warily. He'd only been expecting August.

Paige stared at them in unabashed horror. Behind one of the masks, a chuckle Spencer hadn't been expecting was dark and entertained. William tugged the heavy scarf down from his face and pulled the ends from where they'd been tucked into the collar of his jacket. He threw it onto the counter as August lowered his hood. His disdainful gaze fell on Paige and then scoured over to Spencer. Even through the thick wool protecting most of his face, Spencer could see his jaw tighten.

"I'm sorry," he murmured.

"Sorry?" William barked. "What the hell for? Been ages since I've had the excitement of covering up a slaughter. And high too… I underestimated this new kid."

August rolled his eyes and tugged the scarf away from his face.

"Thomas," August insisted. "His name is Thomas, and you would do well to not be so fucking amused, Will. Did you bring the gun?"

William waved a hand and didn't bother to look at them. He unbuttoned the heavy coat and ambled towards the back of the coffee shop, tossing the coat aside as he went. Paige stared between them, panic mounting.

"Gun?" she demanded. "Who the hell are you people? What has Tom gotten messed up in?"

Spencer grimaced as August rounded on him.

"Aug, this is Paige. She's a friend of Tom's. She's twenty-four, makes jewellery and stuff," he replied with a sarcastic grin. "And believes that if you know personal information, you won't kill her."

August did not look amused. Spencer shrank under his glare.

"I said I'm sorry!"

"Sorry, Spencer? You say you are sorry when you break a vase, not when you send a new vampire on a massacre!"

"What did you want me to do?"

Spencer slumped down into an armchair, burying his face in his hands. He'd never felt worse about letting August down. It made his stomach churn and clench. Seeing that look in his eyes was painful. He couldn't see it again.

"Your job, Spencer," August hissed. "You were supposed to look after him."

"I tried."

August huffed and Spencer heard his footsteps leading him further into the coffee shop. He let out his breath through his nose, pressing his fingers into his eyes. This never would have happened if August was looking after Thomas, if it had been anyone else. They would have known to look out for junkies.

People on drugs smelled amazing. The endorphins and chemical highs in their blood gave off the most fantastic scent. Preoccupied with helping Thomas learn how to corner someone, he'd not even been thinking about the other dangers.

"What's... what's going on?" Paige asked.

Spencer lifted his head. There was no point in wallowing. If he didn't help sort this out, things would only get worse. He needed a solution. He needed to help and not look completely useless. What did he need to do?

"Paige, is there anyone else due to be at work today?" he asked.

She shook her head.

"No, it's just me."

"Alright. I want you to write a note. Say there was a personal emergency and you won't be open today. Stick it to the inside of the glass. Do not open the door."

Paige gulped and nodded, making her way behind the counter as Spencer followed August and William towards the back room.

William pounded a steady beat on the door. His foot tapped the same rhythm on the tile. He hummed and rocked his head from side to side.

"Come out, come out, little newbie," he sang in a low, rough voice. "I'm just beginning to like you but if you keep me waiting, I'll have to break all your fingers."

"Is that really necessary?" August asked.

"Well, I suppose I could break down the door," William suggested idly. "Unless you'd like to sire a locksmith?"

The look August gave William was full of such fury that Spencer didn't dare say anything. He hung back from them, watching the door, listening for sounds from the other side.

"Spencer," August said after a moment. "Get the girl."

Spencer hesitated. He wasn't entirely sure how August thought Paige would be able to help. However, out of a choice between getting her and waiting for William to decide to break all of Thomas's limbs, he turned and went back to the front of the coffee shop.

She was sticking the note on the inside of the window. Sunlight streamed through the gaps in the blinds and Spencer kept his distance.

"Paige, they need you round back."

She didn't move and he knew she had heard him. Frozen in place, she stared longingly through the gap in the blinds and let out a heavy breath.

"Come on, it'll be alright."

Nodding, she stepped away from the window. The blinds slid back into place, blocking most of the light but lines of sun stretched across the floor. Even if they got Spencer from the back room, how the hell were they going to get out of here?

Spencer led Paige back to the door to the supply room where August and William were waiting. William had resumed his banging on the door but he watched with interest as August stepped forward.

He didn't say a word and the hairs on the back of Spencer's neck stood on end. Paige looked between the three of them but she couldn't move fast enough. August snatched her wrist, pulled it to his mouth and turned his head quickly. Paige shrieked as a long red gash along her wrist began spewing blood.

"What are you…"

"Thomas!" August snapped loudly. "You smell that?"

He grabbed Paige by the back of the neck, forcing her down, her wrist pressed against the bottom of the door. The smell would certainly reach the new vampire. Fresh blood always did.

"You will open this door or the next thing I rip open is her throat."

Spencer could hear a shuffling and William was almost bent double in silent laughter.

"I am not kidding. The girl smells good and I've not fed," August said bluntly. "Open – this – door."

Paige sobbed and shrieked, trying to wrench herself from August's grasp. Spencer shifted his weight back and forth. He'd promised to look out for her. He'd said it would all be fine.

"On your head be it," August said, pulling Paige upright. "Any last words, Paige, right?"

"Please... please don't..." Paige sobbed.

On the other side of the door, Thomas let out a strangled cry of frustration. Something heavy hit the wall and the door was wrenched open as August brushed dark hair away from Paige's neck.

"Don't!" Thomas cried. "Don't kill her!"

August glanced between William and Thomas and released Paige. She hurled herself away from him, clutching her wrist, trying to slow the blood.

"That is how you get a vampire out of a locked room," August said triumphantly to William.

Thomas clung to the door handle, wavering unsteadily. Blood was smeared across his lips and chin. His arms were coated from fingers to elbows, red handprints on the walls and door. A large stain had soaked down the front of his shirt, blood and sweat mingling together. His eyes were wide and alarmingly blank as he stared at them. They stared back, taking in the sight of the newest vampire.

William was the first to snap out of the shock. He scoffed and grabbed Thomas around the middle. Shoving Thomas face first against the wall, he pinned his hands behind his back.

The floor was littered with bodies and Spencer could see that while Thomas's aim might have improved, his technique had not. Necks were shredded, arms torn, and bits of stringy flesh spattered the floor. The smell was so strong that even Paige gagged and covered her mouth, blood spilling from her wrist and making tracks down her arm.

"Spencer, kill the girl."

"What?"

"NO!"

"Please!"

August glared at Thomas. The young man's eyes were alight in fury and panic. He struggled with no success.

"You can't!" Thomas shrieked, kicking back at William's shin. Drops of blood splattered against the wall as he shook his head and tried to wrench himself from William's grasp. "You can't! I'll kill you!"

August stepped forward and took hold of Thomas's chin.

"What I can and cannot do, young one, is not for you to decide. You have revealed us to a human. You think she'll sit by and not tell anyone?"

"I won't!" Paige cried. "I promise."

"August, come on," Spencer hissed.

"Do not test me, Spencer!"

"I'll kill her," William said, releasing Thomas.

He'd only managed to turn around before Thomas hurled himself at William's back, arms locked around his neck. He was no match for the larger man, who slammed Thomas back into the wall.

"Just stop, please!" Spencer begged.

Reaching out, he took hold of August's arm and dragged him back.

"August, please. Don't kill her. She's not called the police. Thomas cares about her. If you do this, he'll never trust any of us again."

August glared past him at Paige, his teeth grinding together. He took a deep breath. Spencer didn't dare breathe. Between Paige's scent in the air, and the stench of stale blood, he was having enough trouble concentrating as it was.

"Fine," August snapped. "You will stay with the girl while we deal with this mess."

"Thank you," Spencer said quietly.

August rounded on him, grasping his shoulder and shoving him backwards.

"God help me, Spencer, you fuck this up and it will be your blood I'm spraying across the walls."

Spencer shrank away from the distant and furious look in his eyes, collecting Paige he moved quickly out of his sight. He couldn't look at August again. That man was not his August, the one who tormented and teased him. It was not the friend who had helped him through his transformations or the lover who had lain in bed with him until the moon rose. The pain that shot through his chest was nothing to do with fear. It was empty, cold, and entirely consuming.

Somehow, even though he'd never felt it when he was alive, he knew that pain was grief.

17

Thomas grabbed the duvet and tugged it up to his chin, rolling forward onto his stomach and burying his face into the pillow. It was too bright in the room, the bed too comfortable, and he wished that he could go back to sleep. Awake, his stomach rolled and churned, threatening to upend itself. His head thumped and throbbed and his hand was sore, though he wasn't sure of the reason for the latter.

His dreams dripped from his memory. A blonde corpse had danced for him, urging him further down a dark corridor. Blood swirled and rippled around his ankles with every step and every sniff of air had the scent of cinnamon, elderflower, and finely brewed coffee. He couldn't remember where he'd been heading, though it had been so clear in the dream. The corpse turned to him, leaning close. Her blonde hair brushed his cheek.

"Kill the girl," the corpse had muttered in his ear in a voice that did not match the face. The voice was male, it was familiar, it was August.

Thomas threw the duvet back and scrambled from the bed as the memory returned to him. He thrust his feet into his jeans and pulled them haphazardly over his hips as he stumbled for the door. Another wave of nausea hit him, a thousand tastes all in one. Snatches of memory flashed behind his eyes and throbbed in his ears. His vision flickered like a scratched disc, jerking in and out of focus.

He was dancing, his body hot and moving too fast. He was in a coffee shop, the taste of blood on his tongue. He was standing in the supply cupboard and the blood didn't taste good, but he just kept on drinking.

He was salivating at the smell of Paige's blood, fighting every urge he had ever felt as it bubbled to the surface, a soup of desire and need and hunger.

Thomas gulped and steeled himself. This couldn't wait until the feeling passed. It wouldn't go away by hiding in bed. He snatched a t-shirt from the laundry basket with no idea whether it was his own or one of Spencer's. He wrenched the door open and let it bang against the wall, fleeing down the corridor, the shirt still hanging from his grasp.

He reached the stairs, ready to descend, when he realised that he had never been shown August's room. Where would he find him? What if he wasn't here? Thomas stopped, leaning against the bannister as he turned the shirt the right way out and tugged it on.

"You're the new one, right?"

The voice came from above him, making him jump. Lifting his head, he gazed up, his eyes adjusting to the light. Her dark skin was submerged in shadow but he could see her seated in the corner of the first landing up the staircase. She leaned forwards over her knees, clutching a notebook to her chest. Tight, impeccable braids twisted back into a knot on top of her head behind a pair of thick-rimmed glasses. Even from here, now he looked closely, he could see that the glasses held clear glass, only for show. Thomas nodded and took a step up, swaying as pain shot across his temple and throbbed behind his eyes.

"Thomas," he said.

She lifted a pen and stuck the end between her teeth.

"Heather," she replied, though her voice was curious, as if she didn't quite believe her own answer. "Are you alright?"

"I'm looking for August."

"Dressed like that, I'm surprised he didn't just leave you," Heather chuckled.

Before he could think of a reply she opened the notebook and scribbled something down. Thomas took another step up the stairs, craning his neck to see, but she snapped the book closed as fast as she'd opened it.

"Spence won't be pleased if you're stealing his man as well as his clothes."

Thomas plucked the shirt further from his body. He wasn't getting any more comfortable with the fact people could smell things on him so easily. Even he could pick Spencer's scent from the material now he thought about it. It made his stomach roll and he squeezed his eyes shut, trying to think of something, anything, that he could focus on instead.

"I'm not, I'm... August said he'd kill this girl because..."

"Oooh," she cooed happily. "Go on. Some devil dealing? A jealous ex-lover?"

He opened his eyes and stared at her at a complete loss for words. Heather lifted the notebook and opened it to show pages and pages of scribbled notes.

"Oh, the writer," Thomas remembered. "It's nothing like that, just..."

Heather looked slightly crest-fallen but she pointed up the stairs.

"Turn left. Second door on the right."

Thomas leapt past her.

"Thanks," he called back as he raced up the next flight of stairs.

The corridor would have been considered dark with no windows to let in the sun, nor lights lit along the ceiling, but Thomas could see every detail. He noticed, as he counted his way past the first door, that the bulbs had been removed from the lampshades that hung on their wires. All of the doors off the corridor were closed and Thomas stood before the second on the right for a few moments. Despite his desperation to get here, he now had no idea what he should say. August's anger with him and Spencer had been clear enough that morning. Would the time have been enough to placate him?

Thomas raised a fist and struck the door.

It was odd, the way his senses picked up on things now. He could tell that August's curses were muttered as he peeled himself from his bed and stomped across the room, but Thomas could hear each obscenity as if it had been said straight into his ear. He could smell the scent of August's skin that clung to every surface and sheet on the other side of the heavy door. Thomas jumped back before risking the door smacking him in the nose, but when the handle turned, the door was pulled inwards away from him.

August stared at him for a few seconds, his gaze starting at his face before sliding deliberately down onto the shirt he'd plucked from the laundry basket. Thomas twisted the hem in his fingers but August did not comment on it. His gaze returned to Thomas's face and he stared, his eyes narrow and fierce. In that moment, Thomas realised that he was perhaps not who the older man had been expecting.

"I wanted to talk to you," Thomas mumbled feebly.

Now that he stood before the blond, he realised that this was only the second conversation they'd had alone. There had always been someone else there. William and Spencer, or the woman, hanging and dying. The only time he'd spoken to August alone was when the man had dragged him from the basement and told him to enjoy the sun while he could.

"Evidently," August replied coolly.

He did not move from the doorway, nor give any indication that he was inviting Thomas inside. He simply stared, a small flicker of an expectant grin tugging at one corner of his lips. Thomas didn't know what to say. He scuffed his foot against the carpet, his toes burying into the fibre, springy and coarse.

"I wanted…" He stared at the floor before August's feet, trying to will the words to come. "I needed…"

"Yes, I find women often come with lots of 'needs'," August said, almost bored. When Thomas looked at him in surprise, he raised an eyebrow. "You're here to ask me to spare the girl, right?"

Thomas nodded, feeling far more foolish than he had moments ago. There was something about the sight of this man that made him feel like a child begging for sweets.

"Your entire existence has caused me more trouble than any I have ever known," he continued. "I had to perform the clan's *justice* on a woman I have known for over a century, I had to clean up half a dozen bodies from the back room of a poxy little café, and now you ask me to forget all rules about our secrecy?"

The way he snarled the word 'justice' was like it was something disgusting he never wanted to hear of. From what

Thomas had learned from Spencer, August was the one to ensure the rules were followed, though he was not the one in charge. He followed rules just like everyone else.

"Please, don't kill her," Thomas breathed. "I never intended to be a problem and I won't be ever again."

"But however will you learn if your mistakes are not punished?"

"Then punish me, not her!"

August stepped forward and crossed his arms over his chest, leaning sideways on the doorframe.

"I'm rather certain that killing her would be punishment for you," he said casually.

"Please," Thomas begged. "Please, don't kill her."

"And what do you suppose I do about a human who knows about us? A human who could run off and tell everyone they know?"

Thomas bounced nervously on the balls of his feet, staring past him at the drawn curtains. There wasn't a sliver of light shining through them. He'd never see that light again.

"Turn her!" he cried suddenly. "You can turn her. She'll be one of us, she won't be a problem."

August's grasp found his elbow in an instant, yanking him into the room and shutting the door behind them. Thomas stumbled as he was released, catching himself on the desk.

"Don't you remember what happens to those who turn humans without permission?" August hissed. "Or have you forgotten your sire so quickly?"

Turning around slowly, Thomas gazed up at the older man. August's face was fury in ice. Cold eyes and pale skin had never burned with as much anger as they did in that moment. He sneered.

"Though, I suppose you might enjoy that," he said coldly.

"Watching me strung up and bled."

"No," Thomas answered quickly. "I didn't mean... I..."

"Then what did you mean?"

Thomas stared without seeing. He knew the rules. He'd been a witness to those laws being enforced by the man before him. There was no way to turn Paige without someone dying for it and they couldn't let her continue living if they feared she would reveal them. There was no way to...

"Let me do it!"

"What?"

August looked taken aback. He even glanced over his shoulder as if checking nobody was behind him, waiting to pounce and condemn him for conspiring to get around their justice.

"Let me turn Paige," Thomas repeated, quieter, more certain. "You said it, I've been trouble. No one would be surprised. She can live and I'll take her place."

For a flicker of a moment there was a curiosity in August's gaze that to Thomas looked almost like admiration. However, before he could contemplate whether the man admired him for his bravery, or his cunning at getting around him, all trace of it was gone and the blond man was sneering derision.

"Pathetic," he hissed. "You've not even tasted the life you could have and you want to throw it away for some girl who won't remember you in a year?"

Thomas didn't want to argue or sound petulant by saying that Paige would remember him, he knew she would. Instead, he straightened himself up and stared back, trying to hold back his nerves.

August muttered words like 'ridiculous' and 'moronic' under his breath as he surveyed him. Thomas held his tongue. He'd given his suggestion, he'd made his argument. No waxing of justice or mercy would convince the man.

Stepping back to the door, August turned the handle and pulled it open.

"Get out."

"What?" Thomas blurted. "But you didn't give me an answer."

"My answer is for you to get out!" August snapped. "You come in here, ask me to save some stupid little nobody by letting you commit suicide? I have had quite enough ridiculous notions of the freedom death will bring for one lifetime."

"But…"

The door was slammed shut before Thomas could utter another word. A click sounded and no matter how hard he pushed on the handle, the door remained shut. He pleaded through the door for Paige's life for another half an hour before he finally admitted defeat. August could hear him, he knew, but he wasn't listening.

Once and for all, Thomas knew, he was no longer a predator as Spencer had told him. Because of his idiocy, once the sun set August would go and kill Paige. Once night time came he would be a murderer.

18

August waited until an hour after sunset before he telephoned Spencer to ask where the girl lived. They'd been stuck in the coffee shop for the day and who knew how far out the girl lived. Spencer had said it was close, three or four streets on the top floor of an old building. She had thin curtains though, and he wasn't sure how safe he would be once the sun rose again.

Shoving a roll of thick material from their stores into a rucksack, enough to secure at least one room from the sun, August set off the address he had been given. Spencer knew to expect him but not to tell the girl. She would only become upset, and probably harder to manage, if she knew one of the men who wanted her dead was on his way.

The youngest vampire's request played constantly in his mind. August had finally given in, asking William for his opinion on the situation. The man was as blunt and coarse as ever but he had told August what he needed to hear.

Climbing the steps inside the building, he came to a slim door on the top floor. He knocked loudly and waited, listening to the scurry of footsteps and whispered questions. Spencer urged the girl onwards and the door was pulled open. Her curiosity was gone in an instant and she stepped back, eyes wide with fear. August smiled.

"Are you going to invite me in?" he asked.

Spencer appeared next to the girl and tugged the door from her grip, pulling it open wider.

"You can't," she said. "You can't come in without an invitation."

August laughed and stepped over the threshold.

"We can," he said. "It just isn't polite."

Spencer smirked and closed the door behind him. No doubt the young vampire had been amused to trick this girl into believing the silly superstitions about their race. He wondered if he'd told her to hang garlic and ask a priest for holy water as well.

Sliding the backpack from his shoulder, August held it out for Spencer.

"There should be enough for one room, perhaps two," he explained. "Once you are done, go and hunt. You will need your strength."

There was no affection to his voice and Spencer's gaze searched him for a moment before he nodded and opened up the backpack, moving immediately through to another of the rooms in the apartment. He'd been here a while already, he'd probably looked around.

"Miss..."

She stared at him as he waited and finally shook her head.

"Navarro," she said.

"Miss Navarro, would you be so kind as to get me a glass of water?"

She was taken aback, being shown niceties when she was

being held captive in her own home, as she had been in the coffee shop. She took three glasses from the cupboard.

"No, just two," he said. "Spencer will not be staying."

"So, I'm your hostage now?" she asked, returning one of the glasses to the cupboard and filling the others with tepid water.

He chuckled and accepted the glass she offered to him. Striding to the nearest chair, he slid down into it without being offered and rested the glass against his knee, looking around. The apartment was crappy, or more appropriately the building was crappy. Yet she had furnished and decorated it until the poor state of the walls and floor was barely noticeable. Beautiful artwork from every continent adorned the walls, interesting knick-knacks stood on every shelf and surface, different but perfectly matching furniture was spread about the small room.

"You are a designer?" he asked.

"Did Thomas tell you that?"

August shook his head and waved for her to take a seat.

"When you have been alive as long as I have, you notice things. Your taste is exquisite, even in your meagre surroundings."

"I make bits and bobs," she said meekly, sliding onto the end of a thin couch. "When I'm not at the café."

He nodded just as Spencer reappeared in the doorway.

"Both the bedroom and the study are set," he explained.

"Good," August said. "Now, back a decent time before dawn please, Spencer. Miss Navarro and I have things to discuss."

Spencer's eyes narrowed and his jaw clenched but he nodded and left just the same. August smiled to himself when he did not hear footsteps on the other side of the door.

"Thank you, Spencer," August said loudly. The footsteps retreated quickly.

"Are you going to kill me?" she asked after a long silence.

"You must understand the situation I have been placed in, Miss... may I call you Paige?"

"Might as well be on a first name basis with my murderer," she hissed.

"True enough. Then you can call me August," he said before pressing on. "We have worked very hard to keep our existence hidden, Paige. With pop culture frequently obsessed with our existence, you can imagine that revealing ourselves is not beneficial. For one thing we would all be placed in prisons for murder."

"You could get blood from hospitals," she suggested. "Or animal blood."

"Both poor substitutes for our needs," August explained. "Blood from a bag has often lost most of the nutrients it once held, like eating an orange without the vitamin C. Animal blood, while acceptable for short periods, is not sustaining. We cannot be merely carnivores, we must be cannibals."

"So you're going to kill me, then? Your latest meal?"

August leaned back in his seat and sipped his water, watching her over the rim of the glass. She was pretty enough. Her copper skin was smooth and unblemished. Long dark hair was thick and straight. Her body was pleasing, what he could see of her beneath her clothes. If it was lust that drove Thomas to his offer, he could understand why. To him she smelled mediocre. Not unappetising but not mouth-watering either. However, he knew not to underestimate the differences people found in others. Those who were best for him did not suit every taste.

"The young Thomas made a particularly intriguing offer,"

August said finally, moving forward and placing the glass on a low table. Immediately, Paige leaned forward and slid a coaster beneath it. "He asked me to allow him to turn you."

She looked up from the coaster and watched him with caution.

"Would that be appealing to you?" he asked, his voice ringing with amusement.

Paige didn't answer him. She stared at him as she carefully sat back in the couch, grasping her own glass with both hands.

"Is it better than being dead?"

"That depends on your opinion of death," he answered. "For me, yes."

"Can I... can I have time to think about it?"

"Alas, no," he said. "For while Thomas' offer is noble enough, it is impossible under our current laws."

"I'm sorry?"

"Our... group, let us call them, does not allow for new sirings."

"Then how did Thomas...?"

"His sire was killed upon his creation."

Paige's lips parted in a silent 'oh' and she chewed the inside of her cheek.

"Thomas has still offered to do this in order to save you. He is willing to take your place on the chopping block, as it were. You would be turned and he would be killed for his crime."

Paige spilled water over the wooden floor as she jumped to her feet.

"No!" she cried. "No, I won't let him."

August watched with silent amusement. He crossed one leg over the other and peered up at her as she began to pace.

"You can't let him, not if it means his death."

"No, clearly," he agreed. "Though, I admit I am curious as to why you're protecting him. He's a killer. You saw what he is capable of last night. Given the chance, he would kill you just as easily."

She rounded on him.

"He had the chance. He didn't take it," she said. She stared at him, her eyes a fire of fury and passion. He liked her in that moment. "I won't let you kill him."

It was at this that August got slowly to his feet. She took a step back, her calves hitting the table and knocking over the glass of water. She barely noticed.

"I assure you, Miss Navarro, what you will 'let' me do is not important," he said coolly. "You never had a choice in your fate here. Either I allowed Thomas his little love story, or I chose the ending of the story myself."

"Love?" Paige repeated, as if that was the important part of their conversation.

August gave her a belittling smile and stepped towards her.

"Yes, love," he confirmed. "Though I do not know his feelings at this present moment, I would suspect, seeing as he was willing to offer his life for you, that they could certainly have headed in that direction. But, as you say, you won't let him."

Her breasts heaved as he came closer. She glanced towards the door and he could imagine the problem forming in her head. Could she get to the door in time? How many of those pop-culture beliefs were true? Which ones would allow her to escape?

The fear made her heart beat faster, her blood pump harder. He caught the scent again, stronger this time, and he had to admit that she smelled good. It was not the best, nor his particular favourite, but he supposed it was like the difference between Chinese food and Indian curries. One would always be your favourite but that didn't mean you didn't buy the other when the mood for it struck. August tongued the ends of his fangs. He had a taste and a mood for her now.

Paige sidestepped, trying to round the table when he caught her. His arm went around her waist, trapping her arm in against her side. He grasped the other arm and held it still, pulling her back against his chest.

"You can scream if you like," he told her with vicious amusement.

For the briefest moment she was silent, but when he drove his teeth into her neck she screamed.

And she tasted all the better for it.

19

August had left the house shortly after sunset and Thomas spent the entire night waiting for him to return. He stalked the corridors, paced in front of the front door, sat on the steps and stared at the few stars he could see through the city lights. His stomach tied itself in knots and gnawed at him in hunger despite having drained half a football team the night before. He ignored the pain. He wasn't going to risk hunting only to miss August's return. Anyway, he'd not been out without Spencer's guidance and he wasn't about to start now.

A fire of orange and pink lit the sky as dawn approached. He'd moved away from the door after being glared at and stood on the opposite side of the road, watching, waiting. Thomas gazed at the approaching dawn over the roof of the house, remembering the saying his mother had taught him. 'Red sky at night, shepherd's delight. Red sky in the morning, shepherd's warning.' He wasn't entirely sure what a red sky was meant to warn shepherds of, let alone him, and he crossed his arms over his chest and began pacing again, watching anyway. Spencer liked to smoke before dawn. He had his spot out on the balcony with a much better view of the approaching sun. Thomas probably would have been there if he hadn't been waiting but he wasn't going to miss August's return for a red sky and a mouthful of smoke. He didn't smoke anyway, it was bad for you. Death was bad for you too but that didn't seem as important somehow.

It didn't matter. Spencer was not on the balcony. For some reason he was enjoying his cigarette somewhere else this morning. That fact only made Thomas's stomach clench all the harder because he knew that reason was named Paige.

He took a seat on a bench on a small patch of grass opposite the house. His knee bobbed in an irregular rhythm and his fingers drummed against his arm. What if August wasn't returning today? What if he was taking over the watch on Paige and Thomas wouldn't be able to find him until it was too late?

Sure enough, the moment he began failing to formulate a plan, a man appeared at the end of the road, jogging along the sidewalk, blonde hair lit peach by the sunrise. He glanced over at Thomas as he came nearer and, with a roll of his eyes Thomas spotted from his position, he stopped.

"Get it over with, Tom," August drawled. "I've had a long night and I doubt you would like to enjoy the day as a lobster."

Thomas got to his feet and hurried across the road. Shadows spilled and spread the closer the sun came. August stopped at the bottom of the stairs and waved his hand for Thomas to speak. The door opened a crack at the top of the stairs but Thomas paid it no mind.

"You can't kill Paige," Thomas said quickly.

"Oh, is that so?"

He shook his head. He didn't want to anger August and he

knew that the man was perfectly capable of killing Paige. The fact he was so capable of the act was what had him so worried in the first place.

"No, you... you can, I mean, you could. Please don't!"

August brushed his thumb across his bottom lip with a smile.

"I meant what I said. I'll turn her. I'll take the punishment," Thomas insisted, stepping forward. August held his hand up, halting him.

Taking a deep breath in through his nose, Thomas could smell the dry grass, ready for cutting. The open air was fresh and clean. Sweat and skin came from August but underneath that lay something else. There was another scent, another person. After the jokes about stealing Spencer's man as well as his clothes, Thomas wondered for a second whether it was the young vampire he could smell but that wasn't it. This scent was sweeter, softer, feminine, and made his mouth water with the taste of elderflower and warm honey.

Thomas's gaze snapped to August's eyes. He gritted his teeth.

"You saw her?"

"Good, you're learning," August replied with a broad smirk. "After the fiasco with the drug binge, I thought perhaps you were not being taught properly."

"What did you do?" Thomas demanded. He balled his hands into fists, his breath coming sharply.

"You knew I would never be able to accept your offer to take her place, Thomas."

Thomas had never known what it was to see red. He'd always been a calm guy. Driven to succeed, yes, to do his best, but anger had never ruled him like it had some of his friends. He was not the type to get into a bar fight or to bristle and snap back if someone said the wrong thing. Thomas Trent had never felt that blind rage that made him want to kill someone.

Since he'd been turned, killing had been for need, for desire, and for hunger. It had never been for fury.

He wanted to kill August now. The red dawn spread across his skin, flushed and burning as he launched forwards.

August beat one of his hands back but the other found the man's neck. He grabbed tight and clung on. August punched him in the side, bringing forth a grunt of air. Thomas yanked August forward, landing a punch across his jaw.

"Let go!" August ordered.

He wasn't listening. Spencer had called them predators and Thomas understood it now. He was a predator and August had taken what didn't belong to him. She belonged to Thomas. Whether it was as a kill or a lover didn't matter. August had taken her. She was his and August would die for what he had done.

Another punch landed across August's jaw and the man growled furiously in response. Thomas surged forward, teeth bared. A tight grasp locked onto the back of Thomas's neck and pulled him away. Before he could fight the hold or even see who was holding him, the bite that had been intended for August's neck sank into warm, musty, and oddly familiar flesh. His fangs pierced the wrist easily and blood spilled over his tongue, his gnawing stomach clenching in approval.

"Like all toddlers," William taunted from behind him. "Angry and bawling until you give them something to suck on."

Thomas glared at August keeping one hand clasped around his neck as the other grasped William's arm, pulling it harder against his lips. August used both hands to wrench himself free and stepped back and rubbed his throat. August's murderous glare was held at bay by the bigger man and he flexed his fingers. William chuckled and finally released Thomas's neck, patting him on the back of the shoulder.

August looked at the arm in Thomas's mouth, the blood dribbling down his chin, and suddenly laughed.

"Learning from big brother, William?" he asked. William shrugged and grinned.

"Is it done?"

August glanced up at the door, watching, or perhaps listening, and finally nodded.

"I left Spencer. He'll finish it."

William wrenched his arm from Thomas's mouth and shook his hand, blood splattering the concrete.

Thomas gasped and gulped down the air. There was something delicious about the other man's blood. He could feel it pounding through his body, warming his fingers, almost as intoxicating as the drug laced blood. He stared at William, breathing hard, and licked his lips. He'd been so scared of this man and yet he was here to help him. He was protecting him.

"And you're sure the boy will manage?"

August's smirk was almost as predatory as the rage that had flushed through Thomas.

"I taught him, William, and Cleo taught me," he said. "He will do what needs to be done."

"What needs to be done?" Thomas spat. "She didn't need to die!"

He jumped out of William's reach. Instinct drove through his body, telling him how to plant his foot and use it to push off. It told him how to hunch his body, coiling like a spring before he hit. His shoulder collided with August's stomach and as Thomas straightened his body the older man was thrown backwards. Thomas landed on top of him, shifting his weight to rest his leg across August's thighs, his hand pressing down on his throat as he leaned over him.

"I should rip your throat out!" he sneered, baring his teeth. "See if vampires can survive *that*."

Thomas grunted loudly, pain driving through his ribs as August's fist slammed into him. Still, he clung on. Saliva gathered on his tongue but it wasn't hunger that gave him the urge to bite down. He lurched forwards.

The hand came under his chin a moment too soon, wrenching his head back. William placed his other hand against the back of Thomas's head and held him in a vice grip.

"Let him go," he ordered.

"No!"

William flinched, jerking Thomas's head. His fingers slid through his hair and the pressure tightened ever so slowly on his scalp as if the large man was trying to pop his skull.

"Let - him - go," he said again. "I like you, kid, but I'll kill you if you don't do as you're told."

There was fear in August's face, flickers of it that he tried to hide. Thomas felt a deep satisfaction in seeing it and he made sure to grip extra tight for a moment before he let go, allowing William to guide him back to his feet.

Deep purple bruising rose across August's throat. Spencer had said they healed faster than others and despite his fury, Thomas was curious about the fact their injuries showed faster too.

"And here I thought Cleo had grabbed a random," August snarled as he got to his feet. "She chose another pitbull."

William released Thomas and patted him on the back. Rubbing his jaw, Thomas glanced between the two men.

"Too right she did. Girl had good taste."

Thomas snorted and crossed his arms over his chest. The

way they were talking about him made him feel like a child. August glanced at him and rolled his eyes. With a chuckle, William wrapped his arm around his shoulders, leading him back up the steps to the door. August followed, closing the door behind them, locking the warmth outside. Thomas saw him glance up the stairs before he looked at the two of them.

"With that done, there is only one thing left to do."

William glanced up the stairs too as he nodded and Thomas wondered what was up there that had them both concerned. Their expressions were stony, almost cautious. Thomas stayed close to William.

August smiled dangerously at the other man. For the moment it seemed like Thomas had been completely forgotten.

"Brother, I'm going to need your help."

20 Behind the Bar

The scent of blood hung heavy in the air. Knowing that he would be kept here for a few days, Spencer wished that August had been cleaner about it. The man could kill without spilling a drop and yet sprays and puddles littered the apartment when he had returned that morning. He wondered if August had done it to torment him.

His body growled the protest at not feeding. He'd tried searching the apartment for food, anything that might keep the hunger at bay, even if it wasn't useful to keeping his body going. It didn't work. The longer he stayed in the apartment, the worse the stench became, even after he'd cleaned meticulously.

She was on the bed. The blankets were flung back, she was stripped naked, and her dark hair spread over the pillow. Though he knew the consequences would be severe, if not dangerous, he had considered drinking more from her a couple of times. There would still be some left.

August's scent was not nearly as strong as hers. She'd lived here for a long time and her taste was on everything in the apartment but August was still there. Spencer had thrown a blanket over the chair August had sat in, hoping to muffle the taste in the back of his throat. He'd thrown the glass he'd used in the trash and shut the bag in a cupboard. Still the blond wouldn't leave his system, the look of disappointment and finality in his eyes.

He didn't know why he was still following his instructions. He told himself that it was self-preservation. August practically controlled the house, if he made another wrong step, he might be thrown out.

Hearing the change in breathing, Spencer pushed himself off the bathroom floor and went through to the bedroom. She sat up, drawing her knees to her chest and hunching over them.

"How long?" she asked groggily.

Spencer checked his watch.

"Thirty-six hours."

She rested her forehead against her knee and nodded into her skin. Spencer sighed. He'd gotten up for this? He'd come in here, where the scent was the worst, just to be asked how long it had been. He could have been sleeping. He could have locked her in here and checked on her the way August had done to Thomas. What did it matter how long it had been? He'd already told her before that he couldn't do anything until she remembered.

"You said it could be any time, right?"

"Different people take different amounts of time," he told her again. "I took two days. Thomas took three. It'll be when you…"

He stopped, staring at the thick material he'd used to block the windows. He scratched his cheek, chewing the inside of his lip.

"When I what?" she asked, lifting her head.

"We had this conversation after August bit you," he said quietly.

In the corner of his sight, Paige nodded and leaned further forward.

"So?"

"So... you remember me saying it."

"It was only six hours ago, of course I do."

Spencer leapt over and landed next to her on the bed. She squeaked and jerked away as he grasped her arm, pulling her towards him.

"You didn't before. We've had the conversation about how long it would take three times. You've woken up, been confused, had the conversation with me, and collapsed again." He rocked his head from side to side. "Except last time you took your clothes off because you said it was far too hot in here. But my point is this time you asked me how long it's been."

She stared at him, incredulous, and took a moment to think about it before she nodded.

"So it's time?" she asked.

Spencer nodded slowly, staring at his own feet.

"I guess so."

"You don't sound very confident."

"I've never done this before."

Spencer remembered how awful he had felt during those first few days. Paige had only been a day and a half, she had to feel like... well, like death warmed up. Yet she laughed. When he looked at her, she was practically glowing.

"Can I say I took your vampire virginity?" she asked,

breaming. "Vampginity, or virgirism?"

He snorted. Even half-dead the girl was funny. Perhaps that was what had made August decide to turn her instead of kill her. Maybe it was why Thomas was so adamant to save her. Either way, it was up to Spencer to finish the job.

"Vampginity," he agreed. "Though, I'm not sure whether you're taking mine, or I'm taking yours."

"Perhaps both."

Spencer brought his hand up and dragged his teeth across his wrist. A thin gash opened up and blood dribbled from the artery. Perhaps if he'd fed more recently it would have been easier for her. But then, he didn't remember taking much from his sire. The guy had been bled for two days, there couldn't have been all that much left. He'd never stopped to ask before. There was no point, not when he never thought he'd be sitting here. He held out his hand to Paige.

Blood oozed across his skin and she glanced at him before taking hold of his hand. Her fingers were soft and cool and even as she drew him towards her with caution, her thumb stroked back and forth against his palm. He was supposed to be comforting her, bringing her through this, and yet he felt like he was being led along. It reminded him painfully of Cleo and her gentle persuasion.

She didn't suck at first. She held him there, her lips pressed over the wound, soft and surprisingly warm. Her gaze met his and she locked him in place, unmoving, just gentle breath through her nose that washed against his skin. The first swipe of her tongue tickled. She used only the tip, like a lover would pry lips apart to deepen a kiss. The second was more confident and he felt the first pull against his skin. She drew a groan from him as easily as she drew blood.

The taste August had allowed him of her blood had been

enough to lock her into allowing him to complete the siring. She had been given August's blood before he finished his part and Spencer's now. They had both drank from her. August claimed she would be sired to both of them. Spencer hadn't thought it would work until now, until he could feel her. He swelled with the urge to protect her, to make sure that her blood was never far from his. She bore into him and with each pull of his blood, her expression was changing. Caution had dripped away. Her features were redrawn over the faded skin in loyalty and desire.

She pulled away first as Spencer's breath came quicker, his eyes cloudy. She was breathing hard and she stared at him with a look he remembered. It was a look August had given him before, possessive and protective, before he'd disappointed him and been cast aside.

"Spence," she whispered.

"Uh huh…"

He was barely thinking, lost in that look as she moved closer to him. Her arms were around his neck before he was able to force himself out of it. He leapt back, launching himself off the bed, and rounded on her.

"Paige, you need to stop," he announced in as firm a voice as he could manage.

She pushed herself up onto her knees, scooting across the bed towards him. She was as perfect as he could imagine and it was a great effort to stop his body from becoming firmer than his resolve. Reaching to him, she took hold of his wounded wrist and lifted it towards her again.

Spencer jerked away.

"Think about Thomas!" Spencer said quickly. "Thomas. You did this for Thomas."

She shook her head.

"But you turned me," she whispered. "You and August. I want to be with you. We'll be together. Come on, you know you'd enjoy the three of us."

"No."

He would. He knew he'd enjoy it. August had already discussed sharing and the idea thrilled him. The aftermath, on the other hand, would be a lifetime of awkwardness.

"No!" he said again.

"Why? I belong to you just as you're mine. You won't leave me, Spencer, I know you won't."

"No, not leaving," he repeated. "Just no... sex. Brother, alright? I'm your brother, or your dad, or something weird like that. Familial love!"

He found himself trapped against the wardrobe as she climbed off the bed and advanced on him. He cursed and tried to open one of the doors behind his back to pull out some clothes for her. It was the nakedness that was making this worse.

Why the hell hadn't August warned him about this?

"But you're not my brother, Spencer," she said, sidling up against him.

Grasping her shoulders, Spencer pushed her away and held her at arms-length. She gazed up at him, that possessive passion in her eyes, and he almost crumbled. Was it so hard to think that he'd last received that look from August days ago, not weeks or months? It felt like it had been months, like perhaps he'd never really seen it at all. The hollow in his stomach told him that he'd lost it and it wouldn't return. Maybe it wouldn't be so bad, giving in to her? The thought thrilled him but opened up the hole even further. It would be a betrayal to Thomas and to August. He couldn't. He shook himself and stared resolutely over her head. At least she was short.

"Remember Thomas," he told her. "Thomas wanted to turn you. He wanted to be with you."

Her anger flared as passionately as desire. She flung his hands from her, striding past him and only turning back at the door.

"Why didn't you let him do it then?" she demanded. "Why make me want to be close to you if your intention was for me to be with Tom?"

Unfortunately, anger made her look even sexier. Spencer had to stare at the wall.

"I'm going to protect you, Paige," he said through gritted teeth. "I will be everything you need me to be."

"Then why not Tom?" she demanded again. "Why not let me feel this close to him?"

He met her gaze then and he gulped. It was cruel, turning her and creating a bond with her. It was cruel of August to connect her to them both. It was cold to demand this of him and yet he couldn't find himself hating August for the decision. He couldn't fight August's influence in his life any more than he could tell Paige to stop looking at him like that, to stop seeing him like that.

That boy downstairs loved her just as powerfully, it's what the sire bond does.

He remembered August telling William, reminding him of the power of a sire bond. Spencer had once asked what was so dangerous about it, why loyalty was such a bad thing. August had told him that it wasn't loyalty, not true loyalty. The sire bond was power. It was control over another person, an unbreakable connection. Even if Paige had decided she didn't want to be with Thomas, if he'd sired her, she wouldn't have a choice in her need to be close to him. She'd need to please him, to not disappoint him. She would be bound more tightly than any slave.

"With Thomas as your sire, it wouldn't be your choice," he said, realisation sinking in. "Being with him would be… it would be as natural as breathing but not nearly as honest. You'd be with him not because you want to or because you love him, but because you need it."

Spencer stepped back and sat on the corner of the bed. The hollow in his stomach was filling with lead and squirming eels. Weight hung inside his body. He could feel the pull and the desire, the hunger to do anything he could for Paige. But she wasn't the only one. Another weight pulled at him, deeper and older.

"August got me to turn you so that you wouldn't be bound to Thomas, so that it would be an equal relationship."

He stared down at his hands clenched in his lap. Telling Paige why August had not let Thomas turn her had awoken something. It had made him truly look at it for the first time. Hardly anyone knew sire bonds and what they felt like. He'd never thought to ask. There was no point, was there? He wasn't bonded, his sire was dead. That was what he'd been led to believe. Now, the closer he looked, the clearer he could see the shackles August had tied around him.

21

The sun was rising outside and yet the inside of the apartment on the top floor was dark as midnight. August took every step with care. This was not a place for stomping around. Unlike the bottom three floors where there was activity in every hour of the day in one way or another, the top floor gave off the quiet reflection of a church or library. This was a home made for the quiet reading of dusty books.

The scent of polish clung to the silver frames and ornaments. Spindly, intricately carved furniture looked like they had never been used for their true purpose, merely positioned to give the impression of grandeur and class. Every time he stepped inside he was reminded of his childhood, though this was no place for a child. Just like his own home had not been designed for a rambunctious young boy.

August lifted his head a little higher as the door clicked closed behind them. Perhaps it had been his years of watching staff come and go as silently as air but the noise irked him in a place like this. He glanced over his shoulder.

William did not seem perturbed by the disturbance. In fact, his expression was not as icy as usual. He gaze darted around the apartment he rarely visited with interest but when he stopped next to August, he was as still as stone. Usually, August might have watched him, looking for some sign of weakness he probably wouldn't find. Not today.

"William, my dear, dear boy. How infrequently you visit."

Charles sat in his usual chair. A large book was open in front of him and an oil lamp flickered on the corner of the desk. He drew his hands back from the volume and lay them delicately along the arms of his large chair. It was the only item of furniture that looked at all used.

August had often wondered if Charles missed the old days. He was never anything less than impeccably dressed, the way a proper gentleman should be, and he surrounded himself with classic design and style. Seeing him read the slab of a book, he looked as if he were sitting for some historical portrait.

William cleared his throat and stepped forward before he spoke. How quickly they all became ghosts of their former selves around the oldest among them. William clasped his hands behind his back and straightened his stance. The lack of uniform did nothing to detract from the soldier standing between them.

"Of course," Charles repeated.

The smile he offered William may have spread to his cheeks but with the loose skin, decaying after so long, it was impossible to tell. One thing was for certain, the smile did not reach his colourless pinpricks of eyes.

"Yet you come now," he continued when William did not speak again. "Always at the end of a leash, my dear boy."

"I am no dog," William answered briskly. Behind his back, his hands clenched and flexed. He rolled his shoulders back and August heard a distinctive cracking of joints.

Charles' gaze landed on August just long enough for him to feel the stare shoot straight through him before the older man's attention returned to William. August wasn't surprised that the man chose William for his interest. August had been up here many times. It was probably quite rare that Charles saw someone other than the person bringing him blood.

August glanced around. Sure enough, an empty blood-bag lay in a waste paper basket and a tall silver goblet stood on the mantle next to the handle of an ornate sword Charles boasted to have come from the court of some French monarch.

"My dear boy, you have been a dog as long as I have known you," Charles said cordially, as if telling him he was intelligent or handsome. "A vicious dog, hard to control, for sure, but you always come when your leash is pulled."

William's teeth ground behind pursed lips. He said nothing.

Nerves pricked beneath August's skin. He wondered if Charles knew his choice of phrase would unnerve him. They'd agreed it would be best if the truth was kept from the young and August had done his part. He had lied and manipulated to keep their secrets hidden. From the smirk on Charles' lips, he knew exactly how the conversation would rattle him. Perhaps it would even drive a wedge between himself and William once the younger man learned the truth. Perhaps, but that was a question for another day.

"First, the army taught you to heel and obey. Then Cleo took that leash and let it out. She used those commands to send you off and kill for her amusement. True, she gave you more freedom, but when she called you still came to heel did you not?"

August gulped back the saliva gathering in his mouth. He didn't know why he was allowing this charade of a conversation to continue, yet he couldn't bring himself to cut it short. Children didn't interrupt in places like this.

"I see your new master likes you on a shorter leash." Charles' chuckle was as loose and sallow as the sections of skin. It tumbled out and broke apart in the air. "No doubt he feels that keeping you close will make you all the more savage when finally let free?"

"Will is my equal, Charles," August said as he was finally drawn into the conversation.

"As I am not?" His voice was calm but August knew if he waded into it, meaning would lurk beneath as treacherous as rocks beneath churning water.

"Exactly," he said, stepping forward to join William.

There was no turning back now. Too many things had been put in place. He had come here with the intention to wade into that treachery. If he didn't it would be his death the moment Paige was discovered. He had not hidden himself behind layers of misdirection and trickery this time. She was his, his and Spencer's, and it would be death to both of them.

Spencer had already confirmed it was complete. Paige was doing well. That was all he'd said in the message and when August had replied, asking for more information, he didn't answer. He'd considered waiting until he knew more but he couldn't risk that word would get back to Charles before he was ready to act. Surprise was everything.

Charles stared between the two of them.

"And I suppose you will pretend to run our affairs in a democracy while you quietly control those you feign to call your equal?" he asked. "How very modern of you."

This time, his laugh was cold and cruel.

"Have no doubt that I am well aware of how you operate, August. Give just enough to assure the illusion of freedom and excitement, but keep them in the dark long enough to fumble and cry for your help, indenturing them to your service."

August bristled and balled his hands into fists. Neither made any effort to move. Charles watched him with the belittling amusement of those who knew they were correct.

"You have had no insight into my operations for a long time," August hissed. "Oh, you knew about those I killed protecting Cleo from your laws, but I have spent a long time surrounding myself with those loyal to me."

"Loyalty is a funny thing. We both know that. It is far more dangerous than it is helpful."

"And yet you demanded our loyalty for decades," August snapped. "Locked up here in your little castle, you have become irrelevant to those you rule. The loyalty they give you is a tradition they blunder through without thinking about it. You are a figurehead, nothing more. I am the one they listen to, the one they fear and follow."

Charles' fingers curled around the edge of the arms of the chair. His knuckles were as white as his eyes. August couldn't tell whether it was fear or anger. He took another step forward.

"You gave me this position, Charles. Now, I am truly taking it."

August saw the tip of Charles' tongue run over each of his fangs.

"I know what your intentions are, August. Had you asked me, you know I would advise against it."

"His intentions?" William asked with a bark of a laugh. "He intends to release the choke hold you've had on the vampires in this city for a century."

August wished he'd be quiet. He'd brought William along for intimidation, not intelligence.

"Is that what he's told you?" Charles chuckled.

"Without you, we will be truly free."

"No, dear boy, you will be truly dead."

His gaze did not waver from August's face and his jaw tightened. August stared back defiantly.

"Unlike you, I plan to lead our kind into the new century, what you've been fearing since you took that chair."

"August," he sighed and shook his head. "You are a smart man, no one has ever denied that, but you are impulsive."

"Impulsive?" August demanded. "I've been planning this for decades."

"You are impulsive. You will lead yourself and those around you to war."

William snorted.

"War?" he demanded. "If we intended a fight against humans, it would not be a war. It would be a massacre."

When Charles turned his gaze on William, even beneath the folds of loose flesh and behind the milky eyes, pity was plain on his face.

"He has not told you anything, has he?" he asked.

No hand was held up to stop him from walking around the edge of the desk. Charles didn't even turn away from William as August reached for the mantel above the open fireplace. The polished handle felt slimy against his fingers. He wondered how recently Charles had tended to the silver and iron in his hands. Taking such care to make sure it gleamed. He had not taken this much care in their survival in a long time.

William didn't move. He watched August over the top of Charles' head. August took a deep breath and Charles stared straight ahead, his expression blank.

"It's such a pity," he said in a breath made of dust and

decades. "Cleo did so love a good dog fight."

The sword cut through the flesh of his neck as easily as butter under August's strong swing. His ear hit his shoulder and his head tumbled to the floor. A puff of dust came from the rug to be immediately drenched in blood. He rolled, nose over skull and back again, staring placidly at the ceiling.

The blade was buried in the wood behind the plush panel on the chair back as the body slumped forward and his blood stained the pages of their history.

22

Thomas hadn't thought to ask why Paige hadn't come back to the house. He had been so shocked that August hadn't killed her like he'd said he would that he'd completely forgotten to ask why he was being given an address instead of being sent back into the basement.

Truth be told he was glad to be out of the house, even without the news of Paige's siring. When he'd woken in the late afternoon it was to find the house in an uproar. He'd considered staying in Spencer's room and waiting it out but the constant flurry of activity could be heard through the walls, the chatter carrying on the stuffy air. He was barely out of Spencer's bedroom door when was accosted by William. The older man grasped him by the shoulder and steered him along to see August despite his protests.

In the bedroom August was the picture of calm. He smirked at the sight of Thomas and explained that Paige had been turned, that she was at her apartment with Spencer, and that they were expecting him once the sun set. Thomas simply stared at him, not sure whether he should thank the man or be angry that he'd been lied to. Instead, he stood until William broke the silence by biting him, teeth going straight through the seam of his t-shirt.

William had only taken a little. He claimed that he should be bonded to his brother and that having someone close would be good for him, new as he was. Arguing wasn't an option, not when the blood had already been taken. Not to mention that he remembered William's threats about breaking his fingers or killing him for disobeying him. Having a brother was better than having a man out for your blood. He'd not asked William if the biting would have to continue if they wanted to keep the bond. In his opinion, that wasn't something brothers did. Not to mention that the wound in his shoulder stung sharply, clouding his thoughts.

It was only as he'd left the house that he'd thought to question it. Spencer had been very clear in the rules they lived by. Sire bonds were dangerous and had to be destroyed. Were the same true of brothers? He didn't even know brotherly bonds were possible for vampires.

Still, it wasn't important to think about that now.

His teeth sunk easily through the shop girl's neck. Her scream pierced his ears like high notes from a violin and the thrilling high at the sound was equal to the rush of pleasure from the taste of her blood on his tongue. The cigarette she'd been smoking fell to the concrete and rolled away. She scrambled at his arms. The pain of her nails in his skin made him draw from her all the harder.

A growl rumbled through his full throat and vibrated against her skin as he shoved her backwards. The back of her head hit the brick with a hard crack and the air, drenched in blood, continued to sing long after her scream had ended.

Breathing hard, Thomas pulled back and released her. She slumped to the ground and the acrid smell of burning hair wafted up into the air. He looked down, let out a low laugh and stepped on the end of the cigarette.

By the time he reached Paige's apartment, the stars were showing as pale freckles across the sky's dark cheeks, hidden under a blush of city glow. He climbed the stairs to her door and knocked, his foot tapping until he heard the latch click.

"Has anyone ever told you you'd be late for a funeral?"

She beamed at him. Her skin looked paler than usual but it made her dark eyes stand out all the more. He could imagine the flush of blood in her cheeks and the flutter of thought of tasting blood on her lips was as intoxicating as the first scent of a kill he'd caught in the club with Spencer.

"I think you mean my own funeral," he corrected, shifting his weight, the warmth of his feed spreading through his limbs.

"You didn't have a funeral," she said.

She leaned on the doorframe, crossed her arms, and looked up at him with the cheeky smile he had often seen behind the coffee machine.

"And you have? If so, I'm offended I wasn't invited."

Paige reached out, grasped him by the wrist, and tugged him through the door into the apartment. Spencer lay sprawled face down on the sofa, his nose and mouth obscured by a cushion. His eyes were closed but he lifted a hand and gave a brief, dejected wave.

"What's up with him?" he asked Paige, not bothering to lower his voice. There was no point. Spencer would hear him no matter how he quietly said it.

Paige crossed the room in three quick strides, tugged the cushion from Spencer's grasp, and promptly thwacked him over the head with it.

"He's moping," she scolded. "Thomas is here now, you can go."

"What did I do?" Thomas demanded, affronted.

"Nothing," Spencer grumbled as he got to his feet.

Thomas noticed the way his nostrils flared, the flicker of fury in his eyes before he managed to plaster over it with another layer of indifference. Paige threw him a look of warning and shook her head from behind Spencer's shoulder.

"I'll be back before Sunrise. I'll bring…"

"August wants us back at the house," Thomas interjected.

Spencer's annoyance was harder to hide that time and he ground his teeth. He scooped up a backpack from next to the door and slung it over his shoulder.

"Fine," he said. "Don't forget to bring clothes."

He was half way through the door when Thomas spun on his heel.

"Spence…"

Spencer paused but didn't turn back.

"Charles is dead. Really dead, not *us* dead."

The sigh that spilt from Spencer's lips hummed with pain and longing. He didn't look back at either of them.

"Of course he is."

Paige watched Spencer walk down the street through the large bay window. It hadn't been covered and the curtains were thin. Thomas could only imagine that this room had not been used much in the last few days. Carefully perching on the edge of the sofa, Thomas took slow and steady breaths, bringing in each scent and focusing on it.

The copper and tang of blood was the most prominent. Paige was everywhere. In the sweet, soft smell of her skin clinging to the couch to the teas and coffees she served at the café. She returned and slid down onto the couch next to him, tucking herself in beneath his hip.

"What's up with Spencer?"

"I'm not sure, exactly," she said. "He won't say. He was fine and then... and then he wasn't."

Thomas frowned but Spencer was quickly forgotten as she leaned closer to him. He grinned down at her and she tucked a lock of hair behind her ear.

"Are you going to teach me to be a killer, now?" she asked.

He almost laughed but instead shook his head.

"It's probably best if Spencer or August does that. They're better at this than I am. I made such a mess that Spencer called me the Zombie Apocalypse."

She leaned forwards and drew her legs up, resting her chin on her knee. The way her hair fell, he could see the smooth curve of her neck. Two marks were fading into her skin. He reached for her and brushed the dark locks from her shoulder.

"I'm sorry I didn't do it for you."

"No," she whispered. "No, it's better this way. Spencer said."

"About loyalty, right?"

"Something like that," she nodded.

Thomas didn't know what to say to that. The air was warm and when he leaned to get a better look at her, he could see more colour in her cheeks.

"Why did it take being turned for you to..." She turned to look at him and found him staring. She blushed all the more. "To notice me?"

His smile was small and nervous. To think, he'd killed a woman less than an hour before with little thought but he couldn't look at the girl before him without feeling tongue-tied.

"I always noticed you, Paige," he murmured, which was only half a lie. "I noticed but I was so busy and…"

He'd always known she was pretty. The first time he'd seen her at the café, he'd considered asking her out sometime. He was new to the area for his internship and figured a date with a pretty girl would be a good way to get to know someone outside of the hospital. But then, he didn't want the date to go badly, which would put him back at square one. Worse than square one, seeing as he'd have to find a new place to get coffee. Instead he focussed on how nice she was, how funny and kind, and slowly that prospect of a date got farther and farther away.

"Being dead kinda frees up your schedule, huh?"

"Not according to Spence," he told her. "Apparently, at some point, you and I will need jobs."

Paige tightened the loop of her arms around her legs and shrugged.

"Well, what about now?" she asked. "Do you have time for me now?"

Thomas slid from the arm of the couch down onto the cushion. Wedged between Paige's hip and the hard, square arm was uncomfortable but he wouldn't have moved even if she'd offered. Her arm pressed a cool pressure against his chest and her hair smothered his lungs in a cloud of elderflower.

She watched him, cautious and hopeful. She shifted and when he slid his fingers into her hair, she sucked away all the air from between them. Her lips tasted of blood and lemon tea mixed with honey. So gentle, so tentative, and yet the taste left him as burning and breathless as his first kill.

"You know," he whispered, honey catching on his lips as they brushed hers. "I might just have an eternity."

23

Feeding had not been as enjoyable as usual. For the first time since being turned, Spencer had found no thrill in the hunt. There had been no pleasure to wipe the questions and suspicions from his mind. Gulping down the blood had been as enjoyable as forcing down overcooked vegetables.

He had stayed out. He had left his kill in a dumpster around the back of a diner and had gone to a club. He'd sat by the bar and ignored the attention a few girls had thrown his way. The thumping music had been a relief to cloud his mind. He knew that he could have killed another easily and yet he was still staring at his beer when the lights came up around the club and the music faded into the drunken chatter of home time.

He considered going back to Paige's place, but knowing August had expected her to be brought to the house, he realised there was little point. No doubt Thomas would have taken her back already. There was nothing in that apartment for him except a scent he could not get rid of and worries he could not forget. He trudged back to the house with two hours before sunrise and headed straight to the back garden, taking a seat on the patio steps.

It still didn't make any sense. For years he had been told that they didn't allow new sirings. It was the one rule that you were not to break under any circumstances and August had been the most insistent on it. Yet he had asked him to help sire Paige. He'd said that by the time she was turned that it would be fine, that he would suffer no repercussions, but Spencer could not figure out how. Thomas had told him that Charles was dead but he'd never been told that the siring ban had just been Charles' law, not one they all lived by. Had August known that Charles was dying?

All that, however, was nothing compared to the thoughts he'd been having about his own siring. Despite the fact he knew siring Paige would be a reason for his death under their rules, for some reason it wasn't that occupying his thoughts.

After almost an entire day Spencer could still not figure out how August had made it work. August had been the one to train him, the one to help him, but he was not his sire. He had not turned him and yet Spencer felt the same pull he felt to Paige, only different. Paige's draw was stronger, purer somehow. While he thought the purity might be because she was new, it didn't lessen the fact he felt something similar with August. He'd felt anger over August, a protective flare he couldn't deny when he was threatened, but he'd never been as mindlessly filled with rage as William had been when Cleo had been killed. Was it simply because August still lived that the bond had not shown itself so fiercely?

Spencer buried his face in his hands and took a deep breath of fresh air. Even outside he could pick up the scents of the others in the house. August's was stronger than all of them. So was William's, now he thought about it. Spencer froze, the warmth in the air settling against his skin.

"Regretting having a kid already?"

William's gruff voice was lighter than usual, filled with a humour he rarely heard. Spencer didn't move except to open his eyes and stare at the grass. William's steps vibrated in the wood and he thumped down next to him. He stretched out but kept a curious gaze on Spencer.

"And people call me sullen."

"Are you saying you're not?"

William let out a snort of laughter and shrugged.

"There are reasons to be sullen and reasons not to be," he said.

He leaned forward onto his knees and rested his head in his hand. He had large hands that still held some of the tan from when he'd spent a lot of his life outside. Spencer had once heard that William had been a farm hand before he went off to fight in the war. The sun seemed to have stayed with him, even though he'd not seen it in almost a century.

"Cleo," William said when Spencer didn't answer him. "Losing Cleo is a reason to be sullen. Being rid of Charles, on the other hand... finding out August is my brother."

"Right," Spencer muttered.

William waited, probably expecting more, but when nothing came, he ploughed on.

"So, what do you have to be sullen about, little boy?"

Spencer glared at William out of the corner of his eye. He was starting to think that he liked it better when William didn't know he existed. Or, at least, pretended he didn't. Digging into his pocket, he drew out his packet of cigarettes and eased one out.

"Are you really giving me the silent treatment?" William

asked when Spencer again held his tongue, choosing to light his cigarette instead of answer him. "I can make you squeal like a pig only using one hand, boy."

"I'm sure you can," Spencer said, smoke billowing past his lips.

"Then what's your problem?"

"Is it your business?"

"Depends on why you're acting like a toddler with his toys taken away."

"And by answering that, I'm answering the original question, still not knowing whether it's actually any of your damned business," Spencer snarled. "I'm not a child, William."

William laughed loudly and clapped Spencer roughly on the shoulder.

"That's debateable," he chuckled. "But, for argument's sake, let's take a guess."

"Let's not."

Placing his fingers to his lips, William watched the swirls of smoke rise up into the air. Spencer found himself watching him, even though he didn't particularly want to have this conversation, and certainly not with William.

"From where I'm sitting, I'm guessing you're either worried you're about to be killed for a Sire, or…" Spencer looked away from him and William laughed. "You're far too easy, little one."

"Stop calling me little one."

"Would you prefer I call you August's latest screw?"

Spencer sat up straight, his teeth bared and his eyes narrowed.

"Don't," he growled.

William smirked far broader than was necessary.

"Ah, so it's August's doing then, this little sullen streak."

He leaned back onto his hands and was silent for a few moments. Spencer stared resolutely across the grass.

"Is it because he dismissed you or because he made you care that he did?"

Spencer sucked in a lungful of smoke and choked on it at William's question. He turned to the older man, his eyes wide as covered his mouth and hacked out a cough.

"You know?" he spluttered. "You know what he did to me?"

"That he's your sire? Yeah, I about figured it out."

"My sire was killed," Spencer corrected. "When I was turned. I remember."

"The man who turned you was killed, no one's denying that. But August has bonded you to him, and him to you."

"How?"

William grinned devilishly.

"Ever bitten on him in the midst of… I don't want to think too hard about what you two get up to."

Spencer blamed the recent feed for the flush that coloured his cheeks.

"Sometimes."

"Then I'm assuming it goes the other way too," he said. "It's the sharing of blood that bonds people, Spencer. Your bond won't be as strong as if he'd turned you but it's there."

It made sense. After all, the sharing of blood was how someone was turned, creating the bond in the first place. He wondered whether it was the volume of blood drank that affected the strength of the bond or whether the transformation changed things. He'd not drunk that much from Paige, August had taken most of it, but he still felt her more clearly.

"And he knew?"

William raised an eyebrow and his lips quirked in a half grin.

"Have you ever known August to do anything without knowing the consequences?"

Spencer flicked his half-smoked cigarette out into the grass, breathing out the last of the smoke.

"He knew," he whispered.

"I figured it out a few days ago," William said with a surprising tenderness. "When I asked him, he explained that he's been doing this for a while. He knew that once Charles was gone, he'd have enough loyalty in this house to ascend unopposed."

Now Spencer wished he'd not flicked the cigarette away. He rubbed his palms against his thighs and gritted his teeth. His fangs scraped the inside of his lip and he stared at the disappearing embers out in the grass. He wasn't sure which was worse, that he'd allowed himself to be tricked in such a way, or that he wasn't the only one who August had done this to. They'd always said that they were just having fun but Spencer couldn't deny his loyalty to the older man. Whenever he'd wanted him, Spencer had been there. All it had taken was the suggestion and he caved willingly. He'd never even questioned it.

"He's done this to others?" he asked. "In the house?"

Out of the corner of his eye, William looked concerned as he nodded. Perhaps he realised that he'd said too much because he didn't push it any further. He didn't make a snide joke or call him 'boy'. He sat silently and didn't move until Spencer got to his feet. He looked up at him then.

The dawn wasn't yet approaching. He had at least an hour. Turning on the spot, he began pacing, focusing on the feeling of the vibrations his steps created. He needed to focus, he needed to calm down. His skin was warm, too warm, and he both regretted feeding and wanted to feed more. Losing himself to the chase would be good. It would allow him to stop thinking for a while. He wanted to stop thinking.

"You alright, Spencer?" William asked.

"He did this," Spencer hissed. "He *did this* to me. He manipulated me, made me like this. I didn't have a choice."

Thoughts spiralled around his head with things he'd not thought about in a long time. Memories of obsession and need, times of desperation. It hadn't mattered that he'd been manipulated back then. He didn't care as long as he got his release. Was that why he was so upset now? Because August had dragged him into this addiction and then cut him off?

William climbed slowly to his feet. His eyes were narrowed, his lips set tight, and he kept his distance despite the fact they both knew a fight between them would only end in one way.

"Spencer, calm down. You're working yourself up to thinking this is something worse than it is."

Spencer spun on his heel.

"Don't you dare!" Spencer snapped fiercely. "You almost killed August when your sire bond ended so you know what it does. Don't tell me I should calm down."

William held his hands up and stepped backwards down the stairs.

He raked his fingers through his hair and gripped it at the back of his head. August had dismissed him, he'd made it clear, and despite the fury there was a part of him that wanted to do whatever he could to stay close. Spencer gulped. How many others in the house felt this every day, knowing that August was done with them? He had their loyalty, he had their bond, and now he was free to move on to the next.

He'd done this to Paige.

Spencer was through the door before William even thought to follow him. His feet felt light as he ran through the house. He leaped up the stairs towards his bedroom. Behind him, William demanded that he stopped, that he calmed down, that he took time to think about it. Spencer wasn't interested. He didn't try to block William from his room, nor did he tell him to leave. He grabbed a back pack and stuffed it with clothes while William watched.

"What are you doing?" he asked. "You can't be serious."

Grabbing a hoodie, Spencer shoved it into the bag and zipped it closed before turning to William. It didn't matter how much he had ignored him, he would need to acknowledge him now. William barred the path and glared down at him.

"Act like a fucking adult, Spencer," William snarled.

"Get out of my way, William."

"No."

Spencer barely took a breath.

"Get out of my way or kill me. I'm not staying here."

"I'll force you if I have to."

"Why? Why do you care?" he asked. "I'm August's toy, not yours. Let him do his own dirty work."

"You're overreacting."

"He's been using me for almost six years. He could have told me and maybe I would have been alright with it, but not like this."

"You're still bonded to him," William said calmly. "It doesn't matter if you leave, that won't end just because you don't see him."

Spencer had had enough. William didn't stop him as he shoved past him out of the door.

"No, it won't stop," he agreed. "But it might stop me from killing him."

24

The streets were quiet in this part of town. His footsteps echoed against the walls of the close built rundown buildings. On one corner a woman smoked a cigarette and gave him an appraising look. On another, two men hastily broke apart as both shoved their trade into their pockets. It had been a long time since he'd been here but it was the only place left that he could think of.

He'd tried all the regular haunts, the places he knew Spencer liked to go when he was alone and the clubs he frequented when he craved a little fun. He hadn't been in any of them. He couldn't even find his scent in amongst the crush of people, something he could always find when he needed.

It had been just before dawn when William had found him, explaining that Spencer had packed a bag and gone. At first he'd thought that Spencer was simply worried about the ramifications of helping to turn Paige. He'd tried to talk the worries down and assure William that Spencer would be back when he realised, but he had been corrected. It had not been the siring but August's actions that had driven the young man away. His trickery and manipulation.

He'd wanted to set off then to find Spencer but the sun was coming fast. Confined to the house, there was nothing to do but worry. He knew that Spencer couldn't have gone far. William said that he'd left an hour or so before sunrise and he'd have to seek shelter. Perhaps he'd gone back to Paige's apartment. It was the first and most obvious thought, seeing as he knew there were rooms protected from the sun.

August didn't sleep. He phoned Spencer every hour on the hour but the call was never answered. He left messages in varying degrees of frustration but he didn't get as much as a text in return. Spencer either didn't realise what was going on, that Charles' death had thrown things into turmoil, or on the off chance he did realise, didn't care.

Thomas brought Paige to see him and August passed her training to William, even if just for a few nights. He had too much to deal with. Paige had asked about Spencer and why he couldn't train her like he had for Thomas. August avoided the question but he could see her suspicion. He could feel it, like he could feel the distance from Spencer. They would know more after the full moon, they'd discuss the arrangements again then.

In the middle of a row of dilapidated buildings the green door at the top of the steps was too familiar for comfort. Flaking paint revealed a multitude of different colours hidden beneath, each as battered as the one that had been used to cover it. It creaked open on a single touch, just the way he remembered. Weeds grew along the edges of the cracked steps and something resembling a cat was in the gutter half way through dying. The building reeked of damp laundry and sheets that hadn't been washed for a long time. August turned back to the street, took one last breath of clean—well, cleaner—air and stepped inside. He didn't close the door behind him and he knew from experience that nobody would care. This wasn't the type of place that bothered with security. If you wanted to keep people out, you padlocked the door or shoved furniture in the way. Luckily, it was not the type of security that would keep him out if he put effort into it.

It had been five years and nine months since he had last been here. It had been mid-winter and the chill spread throughout the building without difficulty. The scent had been different then. Vomit clouded the air. Blood hung in every crevice, drenched in a variety of substances. August hadn't liked coming here and the one he'd sent after him had liked it even less, but it was a necessity. It had been worth it. *He* had been worth it.

He could smell him now, in amongst the less desirable scents. There were people tucked into every room and the murmur of chatter filled his head as he made his way to the back of the building. If he wasn't here then he'd been here recently. Perhaps he'd hidden out the daytime in this hovel, one of the few places truly familiar to him.

The door at the end of the hall was closed but a turn of the handle proved that Spencer had not been trying especially hard to keep anyone out. The wood scraped the floor as it swung open, loose on its hinges.

"Fuck off, August."

August let out a breath verging on a laugh as relief flooded him. He closed his eyes for a moment, glad that this had not been some trick. Spencer knew enough about false trails to obscure his scent if he wanted. He'd taught him, after all.

He stepped inside and closed the door behind him.

"I thought you said you never wanted to see this place

again."

"I said a lot of things."

Spencer sat against the wall, turning a cigarette over and over in his fingers. He didn't look up. August moved further into the room and spotted a small bag of white powder lying innocently next to Spencer's knee on the stained and burned wood.

"Did you…"

"No," he breathed. There was a pause and then "was thinking about it."

August could hear the pain in his voice. Spencer's guilt and regret vibrated against his skin and beneath his bones, tugging and twisting.

"Why, Spencer?"

The floor didn't look particularly appealing but August moved closer and crouched before him anyway. He picked up the clear bag and closed it in his fist. Spencer looked at him then. A smile as bitter and unappealing as the smells of the building on his lips.

"Because, for once, I wanted to be alone in my head," he snarled. "But you know all about that, don't you?"

August gulped and got back to his feet.

"William told me what he said to you."

"What you didn't tell me, you mean?"

"There was no reason to tell you."

"That you forced your way into my head? That you bonded me to you without my permission?"

August snarled out a laugh even though the pathetic twinge in Spencer's voice wrenched his stomach.

"I didn't hear you complaining when you were begging me to bite harder, Spencer" he sneered in return.

Spencer remained as pale as ever but there was a heat of

embarrassment to his skin as he jumped to his feet. The cigarette crumpled and split in his fist, tobacco dusting down like snow.

"You never told me what you were doing!" he snapped. "You were using me. William told me that I'm not the first."

"I've been alive one hundred and twenty-two years, Spencer, did you think me a virgin before I met you? We both know you weren't."

He waved his hand towards the battered mattress in the corner.

August had never seen Spencer move as fast as the punch that landed across his jaw. Snarling, August shoved Spencer backwards and pressed his forearm across the younger man's throat, pinning him against the wall. He was met with loathing and pain in equal measure.

"Get off me," Spencer hissed.

"No! Not until you hear me."

He didn't fight. He stood with his back against the wall and August's arm wedged under his chin. The grit of his teeth was defiant but there was a longing in his eyes, desperation he couldn't hide. August pulled back, instead pressing his hand against the brick next to Spencer's head.

Like when William had come to him, there was nothing left to hide.

"I have been manipulating sire bonds for a long time. Some of them were lovers but not all. Mostly, I chose those who I thought would be helpful to me. Charles held a strong grasp on the vampires here and I... I found it funny to undermine him."

"So I was a joke to you? Some little prank?"

"No," he snapped. "I just said I chose people I would find useful. Just let me explain, will you?"

Spencer grimaced but nodded.

He went to rub his hand over his face before he realised he was still holding the little packet of white powder. He tucked it into his back pocket. Spencer followed the packet with his eyes and licked his lips.

"Cleo and I would choose out of those who were turned. Someone else usually did the deed and I kept myself as Charles' favourite by doling out his punishment. I would train them and in doing so I would share blood with them."

Reaching up, August ran a long thin finger down the side of Spencer's neck. He almost expected for him to cringe away but he didn't. He watched him with a kind of fascination.

"You remember me training you?" he asked. Spencer nodded. "When I taught you how to aim. You bit me then, just a small taste, but it was enough."

"So you just… picked me because I was turned?"

August shook his head. His fingers slid to the base of Spencer's skull and he gripped his short hair. The younger man gritted his teeth but stayed quiet.

"You were different. I chose you. I gave up one of the others I had bonded in order to have you, Spencer."

"My sire…"

"Was one of mine."

Spencer gazed at the wall, his expression blank. August forced him to look at him with a tug on his hair.

"I know you're upset that I lied to you but you have to come back."

Short dark hairs slid from his fingers as Spencer pushed him back and wrenched himself away, ripping hair from his scalp. He slipped past him, further into the centre of the room to put distance between them.

"No, August. You don't just get to tell me you chose me

and then order me around. You may have done this to me but you're not my master."

Rubbing his hands together to get rid of the last of the hairs, August turned around to look at him. He was fidgeting in a way August had not seen in a long time. It worried him far more than it should have done. Spencer wrung his hands and pulled on his fingers. He shifted his weight and his gaze flickered around the empty room. August moved for him but Spencer was quick to jump back again.

"I am not trying to be your master," August said. "But it is not safe for you alone. Things are in motion. Things you cannot understand."

"Because you never told me!" Spencer snapped. "You've kept your secrets and I always ignored it because I... because..."

"Because it was safer," August finished. "Look, please, just come back. I'll explain everything. There are those who are angry about Charles' death and they're more..."

"I DON'T CARE!"

"You need to care, Spencer," he replied, trying to stay calm though desperation was quickly seeping in. "These... *people* will kill you if you're not careful."

"So, because of something you did, I'm screwed?" Spencer demanded snidely. "Do you see the pattern here?"

Spencer snatched up his backpack from the floor and slung it over his shoulder. August jumped forwards and grabbed him by the elbow.

The smile on Spencer's lips disarmed him. The younger man stepped towards him. Barely a breath between them and his hand slid past August's hip. He realised what he was doing a moment too late and Spencer slipped out of his grasp, the bag of powder in his hands.

"Stop!"

"Fix your own problems, August."

The door squealed in protest as it was wrenched open and almost pulled from the wobbling hinges. August launched himself after Spencer but he was storming down the corridor towards the door, a fury in his quick steps. A few curious faces peered out past doors held open a crack, their eyes glazed and bland smiles on their lips.

"Spencer!"

He didn't look back. He quickened his step, swerving past trash bags left in the corridor. August broke into a jog, but just as he was getting into his stride the sight before him brought him to a skidding stop.

Spencer stood at the top of the steps on the other side of the green door. He stared down at six men who had surrounded the entrance. Their heft was nothing to the vicious, proud snarls on their lips.

"August Caine," the one in the centre growled, shifting his attention from Spencer to August. "We've been looking for you."

25

"We've been looking for you."

There was nothing reassuring about the gravel rough voice of the man before them. Spencer's eyes narrowed and he flexed his fingers, taking a cautious step backwards. The men surrounding the steps reminded him of the people dwelling in the building behind him. They had a feral quality. From the glint in their eyes to the sneers curling their lips, he could see their hunger just beneath the surface. He'd seen it so many times on the faces of those gripped by withdrawal that he pitied them for a moment. That was, until the man spoke. These were no junkies desperate for a fix.

Spencer didn't need to look over his shoulder to know that August was there. He could sense the anger, and perhaps the fear, at the sight of the six men. He couldn't remember a time when he'd seen August truly scared. The fact it was there now unnerved him.

"Congratulations, Kaleb," August's words were calm and silky, even with the current of venom that ran beneath them.

"How long did it take you to sniff me out?"

The man on the far right flexed his thick fingers and the one next to him brought a crowbar around from behind him to hang by his side. He tapped the hooked end against the side of his shin in a steady heartbeat rhythm. The man named Kaleb on the other hand, grinned. His dark hair curled to his brow over dark tanned skin. He had bright intelligent eyes but the smile on his lips was vicious, almost canine.

"You drainers make it easy for us," he chuckled. "Confined to your black little rooms for so long."

Kaleb stepped forwards and, next to Spencer, August mirrored the other man. Kaleb was bigger than August, bigger than William, Spencer guessed. His thick neck led down to powerful shoulders and a broad barrelled chest. He'd seen August take down bigger men when needed but there was something about these men that put Spencer on edge. Perhaps it was the crowbar.

"Well, you found me, so what do you want?" August demanded.

Spencer glanced sideways and gritted his teeth at the sight of August. His own anger had boiled to nothing in the face of the six men. Instinct raged and it was telling him to protect the blond man next to him. Kaleb put one foot on the bottom step. He gave a leering grin as he looked August up and down.

"You made a big mistake," he said at last.

Spencer didn't know how August could remain so calm. Behind his back, August's hands were clasped into tight fists, but he projected cool politeness down the steps.

"In killing the old one," Kaleb barked, straightening up.

August cocked his head to the side as he surveyed the man beneath him. He stepped forwards and Spencer jumped to join him, but August's hand came to his elbow, pushing him back.

"What we do is no business of yours."

"You think so?"

August smirked.

"When was the last time I asked your thoughts on anything, Kaleb?"

Kaleb sneered and one of the men moved to join him. Unlike August, Kaleb did not push the man back. The others tightened ranks and Spencer took another step backwards at their advance.

"Those laws have been in place for a hundred years, drainer. If you think we'll take this change lying down…"

"No, not lying down," August interrupted with a chuckle. "But perhaps you'll sit and beg."

The man with the crowbar jumped forward, raising his weapon as he ascended the steps with a snort of annoyance.

Spencer shoved his way past August with a snarl.

"Stay away from us!" he ordered.

The men all laughed. Loud rough and barking laughs echoed amongst the close buildings and down the corridor behind them. Spencer heard one of the doors grind against the floor but he didn't dare look back to see who was watching them. He couldn't risk taking his eyes off the men before them.

"Aww, is the milk tooth scared?" the man snarled.

Spencer was scared. He was scared of who these men were and the fact that he was stepping up to them in defence of August. Was this what loyalty meant when it came to the bonds? However, there was an emotion much stronger than fear coursing through him and he sneered as he looked the man up and down.

"No, you should stay away because if you come any closer I'll take that crowbar, shove it up your ass, swirl it around, and pull out your intestines like cotton candy!"

Kaleb howled louder than any of them as he laughed. For the first time since August had appeared beside him, his attention returned to Spencer. His amber eyes were bright with laughter and he pointed a thick stubbed finger at Spencer, grinning.

"This one has teeth!" he snorted. Reaching out, he slapped the back of his hand against his friend's chest. His smile darkened. "I'm going to enjoy ripping them out one by one. Isn't that what you do when someone breaks the rules?"

He rolled his shoulders back. The bones crunched so loudly that it sent a shudder of revulsion down Spencer's spine. He ascended one of the steps and with a single look, the man with the crowbar stepped back. He kept his gaze on Spencer as he addressed August.

"Your rules change, Caine, and all the rules change. Do you hear me?"

August's calm control was cracking, Spencer could feel it. He could hear the grind of his teeth and see the dead fury in his eyes. He remembered August's roar as he'd cracked under the pressure of William's words back in the house. He remembered being scared of him then. Now, he wanted August to crack. He wanted to see the fury that would let these men know who they were dealing with.

"You wouldn't dare," he hissed.

"You think?" Kaleb was doing a much better job at remaining calm, though Spencer guessed that the five men backing him up had something to do with that. "Perhaps we should take a little token to ensure you behave."

He gave the smallest jerk of his head in Spencer's direction and at once all the men were moving. They closed in leaving no escape except back into the building. Every one of them was on the dirty concrete steps. Spencer gasped in surprise as August took a tight grip on his arm and yanked him behind him.

"If any of your mutts touch him, I will slaughter you all. Do you hear *me?*"

Kaleb threw his arms out to stop the men from coming any closer. His expression was stony.

"This will not go unanswered," he said darkly. "If your ranks swell, we will have no choice but to retaliate. And we're not the only ones. I suggest you bring your pets in line... fast"

Kaleb ran his tongue over his teeth as he looked between them. He nodded his head backwards and the other men retreated down the steps without a word. They apparently didn't need any further orders. Turning, they stalked away, moving together into a tight pack. Kaleb's eyes narrowed and, for a moment, Spencer wondered if he would follow. He did. He jumped down the last step and strode after the others, his long legs quickly catching him up with them.

They were out of sight before August moved. He slumped from his stiff and straight stance and took a step to the side. Slumping onto the low wall, he buried his face in his hands. He was breathing hard into his palms and Spencer almost forgot that he'd been leaving. He forgot that he'd been angry as he moved closer to him.

"What the hell was that?" he asked.

August didn't look up. He pressed his hands to his knees and stared at his boots.

"Aug?"

He pushed himself up straight and only glanced at Spencer. Hurrying down the steps, he waved him on.

"We need to get back," was all he said.

Spencer jumped down the steps after him.

"What? No. You need to tell me what's going on."

The fury was back in August's eyes in an instant. He reached out and wrenched the backpack from Spencer's shoulder. As he snatched to get it back, August grabbed him by the arm and pulled him closer.

"Were you not listening to that conversation, Spencer? Did you not hear the part where they threatened to take you if I didn't make sure everyone behaves?"

It didn't matter how hard he pulled against the grasp, August didn't let go.

"I don't even know who *they* were."

August rolled his eyes and turned away, pulling Spencer along the street. He tripped and fell into stride. He could see curious faces in the windows as they passed. It didn't matter how much they'd seen, nobody would be calling the police. In this part of town nobody called the police unless there was a body, and even then it was a matter of making sure they didn't have anything valuable first.

There had been a time when he would have been watching from the window like the rest of them, wondering. He'd been taken away from all that and while before he'd thought it had been chance, a lucky break, perhaps, he now knew that he'd been plucked from this life. He'd been angry in the house, hurt and confused, but pride swelled in his stomach that he'd not found all this by mistake or circumstance. August had chosen him. August had broken rules and given up another just to keep him, and now he was willing to fight and kill to keep him from harm.

It was better to move away from the prying eyes. Spencer allowed August to pull him along until the end of the road before he yanked back. August had relaxed enough that his arm slid easily from his grasp and he jumped away before the older man could think to regain his grip.

"I'm not going anywhere until you tell me what's going on," he said.

August growled and glanced around. His eyes narrowed and he was grinding his teeth again. Spencer bit back a grimace.

"Stop being a petulant child, Spencer."

"Stop treating me like a child!"

"Oh, that's mature," August snarled.

Shaking his head, he took another step away from the blond and held his hands up in defeat. He'd been leaving anyway. What did it matter if these guys were mad at August. Apparently it had nothing to do with him and August could take care of himself, so why should he stay? If August wasn't going to tell him what was going on, he figured he could just go back to his original plan and get out of town. Yes, the older man had protected him, but he couldn't go on feeling like a child. If he wasn't in town, August wouldn't have to worry about him.

"Fine, see you later, August."

He'd barely turned away before the hand was on his elbow again.

"Spence, stop."

Was he hearing things, or was there a note of desperation in August's voice? He looked back to find the fury had gone from his face. Spencer drew his bottom lip between his teeth.

"Just tell me," he said quietly.

August let go of him and groaned out a deep sigh.

"That was Kaleb," he said, defeated. "He is the alpha of the werewolves. There's been a deal in place for a long time, since Cleo and I first arrived here. We don't hurt each other and we keep our numbers under control. I killed Charles and now they think I'm changing our laws. If we're not careful they'll declare it open season on vampires. And with the full moon in a few nights…"

Spencer blinked and stared at him. He knew August was still talking, that he was explaining things to him the way he'd wanted, telling him things he should know, but he didn't hear another word of it. His mouth opened and closed, trying to form the words he wasn't sure were there. When August stopped talking, he looked at him in a mixture of amusement and concern.

"Spence?"

He finally found his voice. He coughed, clearing his throat as he shook his head in disbelief.

"There… there are werewolves?"

MORE FROM CHELE COOKE

Thank you for reading Teeth, the first book in this series. I hope that you have enjoyed it and are looking forward to the sequel.

Meat, the second instalment of the series, will follow on from where Teeth has finished, following a new set of characters.

Authors rely on word of mouth as a vital part of sharing our work. Therefore, I would like to urge you to leave a review of Teeth via your retailer or a book sharing website such as Goodreads.

All reviews, good or bad, are very much appreciated.

Thank you for reading.

ACKNOWLEDGEMENTS

I would like to thank Rhian and Moa for their support and encouragement in writing Teeth. As always, you two save me by listening to my rambling and telling me I'm not completely insane.

Thank you to everyone on Wattpad who read this when it was just a silly serial I was publishing week by week. Your comments and questions really helped to develop this story.

Thank you.

ABOUT THE AUTHOR

Chele Cooke is a Sci-Fi, Fantasy, and Paranormal author based in London, UK.

Chele is an English-born writer based in London. With a degree in Creative Writing from the University of Derby, Chele has been writing for over a decade, both original fiction and fan fiction. She has a number of other original works, including "Out of Orbit": a gritty, dystopian Sci-Fi series.

For more information about Chele, the "Teeth" series, promotions, future releases, and to receive a free short story sign up to Chele's mailing list at

www.chelecooke.com

Printed in Great Britain
by Amazon